The COB
CAPE TOWN

A TALE OF COURAGE, LOVE, AND TRANSFORMATION

SKIP JOHNSON

The **COBBLER** of **CAPE TOWN**

A TALE OF COURAGE, LOVE, AND TRANSFORMATION

SKIP JOHNSON

Cover and Interior Design by Dino Marino | dinomarinodesign.com

Copy Editing by Jessica Andersen | jessicalandersen.com

Proofreading by Linda Dutro I lindadutro@gmail.com

Paperback ISBN: 979-8-9871654-4-7

eBook ISBN: 979-8-9871654-3-0

"It always seems impossible
until it's done."

—Nelson Mandela

ACKNOWLEDGMENTS

As always, I want to thank my extraordinary team that helped bring this project together: Editor Jessica Andersen, Proofreader Linda Dutro, Cover Designer and Interior Format Specialist Dino Marino, and Web Designer Emily Grimaldi. You are consummate professionals, and I am grateful for your variety of skills.

Additionally, I have come to rely on my Advance Review Team in ways I never knew I would. You are all consistently willing to dig in and help successfully launch each book I write, and it encourages me more than you know.

I am grateful for all of you in helping to bring these stories to the world, and to hopefully make it a better place with each book.

DEDICATION

To Scott and Kathy.

I am grateful for both of you,
and I'm proud to be your brother . . .

Skip

OTHER BOOKS BY SKIP JOHNSON

All books available at www.skipjohnsonauthor.com

The Mystic's Gift:
A Story About Loss, Letting Go . . .
and Learning to Soar

(Book 1 in The Mystic's Gift/Royce Holloway series)

A spellbinding, deeply moving story that is quickly becoming a self-help classic. Following a sudden, unimaginable personal tragedy at a point in his midlife when Royce Holloway thought he had it all, he is introduced to a wise, exotic, enchanting mentor named Maya, who takes Royce on a powerful journey of courageous self-discovery and incredible possibilities.

What he learns on this captivating, often poignant trek across two continents will change him in a powerful way, but you may find that the life changed most . . . is yours.

The Gentleman's Journey:
A Heartwarming Story of Courage,
Compassion, and Wisdom

(Book 2 in The Mystic's Gift/Royce Holloway series)

Five years after that glorious week when Maya shared six life-changing principles from an ancient secret book of wisdom with him, Royce is ready for a new chapter—to push his skills and his life to a higher level and make an even greater impact on the world.

In fact, he feels something is *leading* him to do that very thing . . .

So much so, that when Royce's journey takes him to the spectacular, historical Jekyll Island Club Hotel on the Georgia coast, it doesn't surprise him one bit when he "coincidentally" meets a mysterious, well-seasoned world traveler, a traveler whose life was *destined* to intersect with Royce Holloway's—in an unforgettable way for them both.

Join Royce on this powerful, spellbinding trek full of mystics, miracles, and inspirational stories.

You may find *your* life will never be the same again . . .

The Treasure in Antigua

(Book 3 in The Mystic's Gift/Royce Holloway series)

When Royce Holloway ends up on the magnificent island of Antigua, it's far from a Caribbean vacation. Instead, he finds himself on an incredible journey to locate a sacred, priceless treasure—one that Godfrey Tillman said would deeply impact Royce—and deeply impact the world.

If the carefully hidden prize could ever be found . . .

Along the way, Royce is led through a series of "coincidental" meetings with wise, inspirational mentors from all walks of life, who somehow seem part of a mysterious, bigger plan to guide him in reaching his destination.

Join Royce on his captivating, empowering, and often poignant trek across beautiful Antigua, and as you meet the different teachers on his path, you'll likely find the "student" whose life is changed most . . . is you.

The Lottery Winner's Greatest Ride: A Millionaire, a Young Reporter . . . and a Journey to Find What Matters Most

When Phillip Westford won the biggest lottery in history, he never dreamed there would be a price to pay.

A very *large* price that would shake his world to the core . . .

But just when he is at his breaking point, Phillip meets a mysterious old Irishman named Patrick O'Rourke who claims he knows the secret for getting the distraught young man back to happiness.

That is, *if* Phillip is willing to undertake a trek to find three wise mentors across the globe.

Join Phillip on a magnificent train ride as he shares the inspiring, incredible story of his journey of transformation with Juliette McKelvey, a young journalist who is on her own desperate journey to rebuild her crumbling life.

It's a ride to happiness you'll soon realize . . . you were *destined* to be on.

The Statue's Secret:
The Answers We Seek Can Often Be Found
In The Most Unlikely Places

Prominent Newport lawyer David Langley is a tormented man consumed by anxiety, guilt, and regret as his world falls apart more and more each day.

Until . . .

He fortuitously comes across an ancient Caribbean statue, which is soon verified as one of the most magnificent, sacred artifacts ever unearthed.

A relic that had a unique blessing bestowed upon it for the benefit of its fourteenth-century owner—and for all future owners . . .

A blessing that it seems could finally lead David on a path to a transformed life.

That is, *if* David can find his way to a mystical meeting with three wise, carefully chosen mentors at a remote location deep within the Dominican Republic jungle . . . within 48 hours.

Otherwise, the statue and its remarkable gift will vanish forever.

As David frantically, desperately makes his way to his final Dominican destination and the opportunity for an inspired new life, you'll find yourself enthusiastically cheering him on every step of the way.

Then, at some point you may realize the one who is truly on the journey . . . is *you*.

Hidden Jewels of Happiness:
Powerful Essays for Finding and Savoring
the Gifts on Your Journey

A book of wisdom, encouragement, and empowerment for dealing with life's daily challenges. Let Skip reveal to you the seemingly hidden gifts that are all around us, waiting to be discovered and savored. You'll feel inspired, enlightened, and happier with every page.

Grateful for Everything:
Learning, Living, and Loving
the Great Game of Life

A deeply engaging book that provides a blueprint for using the power of gratitude to increase your happiness and fulfillment. You'll find delightful stories and practical ideas for turning your life into a great game to play each day, instead of a dreary battle to be fought.

TABLE OF CONTENTS

CHAPTER 1

"Mr. Van der Meer, it's time for your medication."

The elderly man lounging comfortably in bed pulled his attention back from the sweeping view of Amsterdam and peered at the slightly open door. An attractive, smiling young woman in a white uniform walked in, holding two pills in her outstretched hand.

Rubbing his stubbled chin, he seemed to be weighing his options, but after several seconds, he consented.

"Unfortunately, you are correct," he affirmed in a faint Dutch accent. "Never thought I would get to the point where I'd need to take these bloody things, but . . . here we are." He sighed.

Taking the two small, pink pills from the woman's soft, lily-white hand, he then put the tablets in his mouth and quickly washed them down with the tall glass of water she presented him.

"I understand, sir," she said with an encouraging smile. "However, your health has been steady over the last few months you've been with us, so the treatment appears to be working."

His brown eyes twinkled. "I suppose you're right. Then again, you've been right with just about everything you've told me since I arrived at this fine assisted living establishment."

The woman grinned. "I do my best, sir."

"Yes, that you do. For someone who is only thirty years old, you're wise beyond your years—and I know there's a lot more I can learn from you. But today, I would like to tell you a story which maybe *you* can learn from." He winked.

The blonde-haired, blue-eyed Isa de Wit cocked her head and raised an eyebrow curiously. "Mr. Van der Meer, I've gained so much knowledge from *you* since you've been here. I can't imagine I could learn even more, but I would certainly like to hear one of your stories today—you know I do love them."

He smiled. "Thank you, my dear. I think you'll find this story to be special. I want to tell you about a man who changed not only me, but the city of Cape Town, the country of South Africa . . . and maybe the world."

The woman sat down slowly in a chair next to the bed as her look of intrigue urged the man to continue.

"There are few people in history who have lived like the man I am referring to. Gratefully, I was able to know him in a way that no one else did. The South African history books never refer to him—the government made quite sure there was little left of his story for future generations. But what I saw and what he inspired in the people there can never be taken away."

She wrinkled her brow in deep curiosity, then replied with a charming Dutch intonation, "I knew you lived many years in South Africa, and I think I may have heard something about this person. Are you referring to the Mandela gentleman?" She then apologetically added, "My knowledge of South African history is not as keen as it should be, I'm afraid."

He shook his head softly and smiled. "No, no, years before Mr. Mandela. This man was the finest cobbler in South Africa, and he was known . . . as The Cobbler of Cape Town.

Isa leaned away, tilted her head, and playfully crossed her arms, unconvinced. "A cobbler? Certainly he wasn't a better cobbler than you, sir. You had quite the reputation for excellence in that field here in Amsterdam."

A smile spread across the old man's face. "He was indeed a finer cobbler than me, and he was also a better *man* than me. What I know about shoes—and life—I learned from him."

As the young woman's interest seemed piqued, Lucas Van der Meer placed two large pillows behind him, then leaned back and turned his gaze out to the city once again. He hesitated for several seconds as if he was retrieving sacred, carefully guarded information. Then he looked back at Isa and said quietly, "It all began only a few miles from this very spot, seventy-three years ago, on a day that changed my life forever . . ."

CHAPTER 2

MARCH 14, 1938

"Lucas, hurry down, you're going to be late for school!"

Aya Van der Meer turned to her husband as he sat reading the newspaper at the kitchen table of their small Amsterdam home. "That boy is going to be the end of me—although I love him more than life itself." She shook her head and laughed.

Looking up from the paper, Rolf smiled. "Yes, he's all boy for sure—and I'm grateful he's ours, my dear."

He stood and put his arms tenderly around his young wife as she laid her head lovingly on his shoulder.

Aya reciprocated the embrace, closed her eyes and smiled. "It's hard to believe we have this life, isn't it? It seems like only yesterday we were in Cairo on our first date. It's not every day an Egyptian girl gets swept off her feet by a dashing young summer-abroad student from Europe, you know."

He nodded and grinned. "I remember it well."

She continued, "Now we've been married twenty years, we have a determined, compassionate eighteen-year-old son, and you have the job of your dreams at the university—plus I get to stay here and take care of our beautiful home."

Rolf smiled. "I must admit, it's all amazing, my love. I . . ."

Right then, young Lucas Van der Meer came dashing into the kitchen. "Sorry, mum. I guess I fell back asleep . . ."

"Again?" she asked, gently shaking her head. "I do think reading books until late is depriving you of much-needed sleep."

"I can't help it—learning about all these faraway places makes me want to travel to every one of them. Plus, there are so many people out there I feel like I can help, and I can't wait to get started!" The wide grin on his face revealed the boy's enthusiasm.

Aya countered, "Right, but we must see that you graduate high school first, and then get accepted at the university. Just be patient, my adventurous son. The world can wait on you."

Lucas's father rubbed his son's head playfully and chimed in, "Now, let's get a move on. Your mother is going to ride with us to school in the new automobile. I understand cars are now more popular in the city than bicycles—and this one is a beauty."

"Yes, indeed," Aya agreed. "Just seeing it in the driveway for the last two days since you brought it home has made me quite eager to try it out."

Rolf nodded. "Very well then. Lucas, grab your apple and cheese—let's get you to school and take mum on this little joyride."

In two minutes, the family was out the door and in the car, beginning a journey that Lucas would never forget . . .

CHAPTER 3

The weather was cold and dreary, and the road was icy on that late winter morning as the family began the fifteen-minute drive to Lucas's school.

With Aya sitting in the back, Lucas turned to her and excitedly commented, "Dad's quite a good driver, don't you think?"

"I am impressed indeed. I never knew your father had so many skills." She grinned.

"Of course you did," Lucas's father joked back at her. "It's no doubt one of the many reasons you married me."

Lucas rolled his eyes and laughed. "Alright, well, anyway . . .Let's change the subject, since you two lovebirds are always talking about how you are so lucky and how you have the greatest marriage in all of Holland. I say we talk about something more important—like your incredibly talented son and how you are going to let him start a new job at the Van Damm Tulip Farms."

The silence was heavy as both husband and wife took in the boy's words. Finally, Lucas's father spoke. "Well, well, this is news to me."

Aya put a hand on Lucas's shoulder, and he looked back at her. "Son, when did you start thinking about this? And are there even any jobs available at Van Damm?"

Lucas's response was swift and enthusiastic. "I've been thinking of ways I could make some extra money. Like you both have told me, travel is the greatest thing in the world, but it does cost money—and yes, Mr. Van Damm says I could start immediately."

"Hmmm," Rolf replied in a contemplative way. "I suppose we did mention something about travel . . ."

Aya looked toward her husband with a smile and added, "Plus, if you and I hadn't traveled shortly after we were Lucas's age, we wouldn't have met, so maybe that's not such a bad idea."

She leaned back in the seat and spoke to Lucas. "Let your father and me talk about it, and we can all discuss it more over dinner tonight."

Lucas beamed. "Thank you!"

Rolf gently shook his head and tempered the conversation. "That's not a 'yes' yet. It's more of a, 'Well, this is a plausible idea.' By the way, where would you like to go if you could save up the money?"

Lucas leaned back and rubbed his hands together as if he were thinking of great adventures . . .

"Africa."

Lucas's mother couldn't conceal her surprise. "Really? You mean to retrace your roots in Egypt?"

"I want to go there someday, but first I want to go to a country in the south, maybe Rhodesia or South Africa. I understand many of the people there are oppressed, and maybe I could do something to help. They speak Dutch in some of those places, you know."

Rolf nodded. "Yes, there's quite a bit of Dutch history there, but it's also an extremely complex country and can be very dangerous."

Lucas fired back quickly, "Father, you have always told me that courage is one of the most important virtues a man can have. I remember from your battle stories that courage was something you had to continually rely on as you and the soldiers helped defend the country. I want to make a difference in the world, too, and something about South Africa is calling me . . ."

Rolf smiled and spoke tenderly. "Son, when I hear you talk about your dream to help others, it makes me so proud. Your mother and I always believed you would make a powerful difference wherever you go in the world—and I have no doubt you will be brave when the time to be so is upon you. We will discuss the journey to Africa as well as the job at Van Damm. There's a lot to consider—not the least being that you must stay focused on your studies."

Right then, out of the mist, a car crossed into the lane of the young family. Rolf's eyes grew wide as he swerved to avoid the vehicle now coming directly at them. With a scream from Lucas's mother and a screech of tires, the new automobile skidded off the road, slid out of control on the icy ground for over one hundred feet, and then collided with a large elm tree, crushing the vehicle.

At that moment, everything went dark for Lucas Van der Meer.

CHAPTER 4

When he awoke the next day, Lucas was lying in a hospital bed on the outskirts of Amsterdam.

He sat up and shouted to the empty room, "Mother!"

A nurse came scurrying in, sat next to him on the bed, and clutched his hand. "Now, now, it's alright, Lucas."

Lucas huffed, "It's *not* alright! Where am I, and where is my mum—and my dad?" His eyes widened as he looked down and saw the dark bruises covering his arms and legs.

The nurse delayed her response. "Lucas . . . there was an accident."

Lucas's face paled, and he shook his head, trying desperately to recall the event. "I remember we were going to school, but . . ."

The woman gently interrupted. "Yes, a car crossed over the line . . . the driver was hardly able to see through the mist, and . . ."

"And what?" the boy asked quietly.

"Your father tried to get your family's automobile out of the way, but he lost control. You were thrown from the vehicle, and it's a miracle you're alive. Your parents—I'm sorry . . . they did not survive."

Lucas stared back blankly, then shrieked, "That's impossible—we were just going to school, and they were telling me I could have a job. Now please go get them—this is a horrible, sick joke!"

The nurse could not hold back her tears. "Lucas, if there was any way I could, believe me . . . I would."

The young man began sobbing uncontrollably, and as the woman instinctively reached out and put both arms tenderly around him, time seemed to stand still for them both.

After several moments, Lucas was able to utter, "What shall I do? Where should I go?"

Her voice quivering, she managed, "Let's talk about this later today. There are . . . options. We will figure this out, Lucas."

His lower lip trembled, and tears continued to stream down his cheeks as he held onto the nurse tightly.

Lucas Van der Meer was about to begin an accelerated journey to manhood that he could never, ever have imagined . . .

Joost Van der Meer received news of the accident and came as quickly as he could from Geneva. It took almost three days due to the treacherous Swiss weather conditions, but he was determined to reach his nephew and settle Rolf's affairs.

When the tall, slim, visibly exhausted man finally arrived, it was shortly after Lucas had been given his discharge papers. Joost walked quickly into the waiting room and saw his nephew slumped dejectedly in a metal chair in the corner. Wearing a pair of jeans and an ill-fitting white t-shirt the hospital had provided him with, Lucas held his papers in one hand, and in the other, he clutched a small bag of toiletries.

Joost removed his brown suede top hat and sat in a chair next to his young nephew. "Lucas, I'm so sorry. I just can't believe it. I wish I could have gotten here quicker. Your aunt and cousins are distraught, as am I . . ." He put his arms carefully around the boy as he noticed the bruises.

Lucas slowly looked into his uncle's eyes, and again, tears began streaming down the boy's face. Joost quickly interjected, "I am going to stay with you for as long as you need me here. We will make all the necessary arrangements, and then we can sell the house, so you won't have to deal with all of that."

The young man couldn't disguise his bewilderment as his uncle continued, "We want you to come live with us in Geneva. We'll make sure you have everything you need, and I want you to know that it's going to be alright—maybe not for a while, but at some point, it will."

The man paused and then added gently, "Let's go to your home now to see what we have ahead of us."

Joost helped Lucas to his feet, then carefully guided the young man outside and into the back seat of a cab that was waiting for them in front of the hospital.

As they rode, Lucas stared numbly out the window at the bleak Amsterdam scenery. After about ten minutes, they arrived at their destination, but the residence now seemed to be horribly sterile and unappealing to him. The same home that had provided so much joy for his entire family all these years now looked . . . repulsive. But he knew he must go in.

Joost paid the driver, and the pair then walked slowly up to the front porch, where they paused and looked at each other, as if they were gathering courage for the next unenviable step of going inside. When they entered, everything was eerily just as it was when the family had departed that fateful morning. Joost took off his jacket and sat down in a brown leather chair in the den, as Lucas walked up the stairs and hesitantly opened the door to his room.

Glancing around his space, Lucas now saw everything through an oddly different lens. Even though nothing in his room had changed . . . *everything* had changed.

Right then, Lucas Van der Meer realized he needed to be out of that house—soon. But he wouldn't be going to Geneva. No, he knew he needed to be *much* farther away . . .

The next week was full of "handling things," as Uncle Joost had said. He did put the house up for sale, and then he went to see a lawyer with Lucas to go over the estate details. It was one somber event after another.

Then there was the funeral. As much as Lucas didn't want to go, in his mind, there was no choice. He wouldn't be able to take the decision back if he chose not to attend, so he went to the service with his uncle, who had mercifully handled those arrangements also.

They stood on a barren hill on that chilly, cloudy afternoon in the cemetery adjacent to the small Dutch Reformed church. Only a handful of people was gathered there, but that is how Joost said his brother had wanted it. Rolf had been a private man, and even in death he wanted just a few close friends there to share that final time with him and Aya.

As he watched men lower the two caskets into the ground, Lucas did everything he could to keep his nausea at bay. With everything in his being, he wanted to turn and run away, but he knew his father would want him to stay and be strong, which he forced himself to do.

When the burial ended, Lucas and his uncle dutifully shook hands with the well-wishers who approached them. Then the affable Dutch pastor said a few kind parting words to them, and the uncle and nephew left to take the ten-minute walk back to the house.

At about the halfway point, Joost's baritone voice pierced the awkward silence. "Lucas, I have someone who wants to buy the house and move in immediately."

The boy did not reply as he continued walking.

"Lucas, I know this is hard. I mean, I really can't imagine how hard it is. But I think you will enjoy being in Switzerland with us. You can . . . make a new start."

Lucas abruptly stopped, then turned and looked into his uncle's eyes with steely determination. Right then, he did not seem like a boy to Joost. He seemed like a man—a man with a mission.

"I'm sorry, Uncle Joost. I am not going."

Joost seemed to freeze, unable to respond for a few seconds. When he finally did, his tone was instinctively firm: "What do you mean? You *must* come with me. Where else could you possibly go?"

Lucas looked away into the distance, hesitated briefly, then looked quickly back at his uncle. "South Africa."

Joost gaped in shock, then he offered a condescending smile. "Lucas, that's ridiculous. You can't go to South Africa. It's at the bottom of the bloody world, plus . . ." His voice trailed off.

"Plus, *what?*" Lucas questioned with an unflappable look.

"Plus, with all the civil unrest there, you don't know what you may find. You don't know *anyone* there, and you don't have a way to make a living. You're just a boy, for goodness' sake, Lucas."

"No," he said, raising his voice and defiantly pointing a finger at the man. "My days as a boy are *gone*. My childhood ended last week on that horrible, icy road. Now I am a man, and whether I like it or not, I have choices to make. I am determined to use my pain and help others who are also suffering. I shall go to Africa as soon as the house sells."

As those words seemed to hang in the cold Amsterdam air, the two turned away from each other and continued toward the family home, falling back into silence. When they arrived, Joost looked at the visibly shaken young man and then pointed to two rocking chairs on the front porch. "Lucas, let's sit down."

Lucas paused, then walked over and sat in one of his mother's wicker chairs.

Joost sat next to him, staring blankly ahead.

He massaged the back of his tense neck, and exhaled. "You are right, Lucas. You *are* a man now. No boy should have to grow up suddenly like this, but that is what is required of you now. It's a cruel event, and I wish I could take all the pain away from you. But Lucas, Africa . . ."

Turning toward his uncle, Lucas narrowed his eyes and fired back, "*Yes*, Africa."

"Listen, South Africa is much different than Holland."

Raising his chin, Lucas snapped, "I know that."

Joost persisted. "Yes, yes, but what I mean is . . ."

Lucas looked again at his uncle as the flustered man attempted to find the words he was looking for. "Lucas, you had a beautiful Egyptian mother and a handsome Dutch father. You are an attractive young man also, but in parts of Africa, especially in the south of the continent, they are unwelcoming to anyone who is *of color*."

As if unfazed by those seemingly harsh words, Lucas responded evenly, "Then maybe I will change things there. My parents always told me I could change the world if I truly believed it—and I *do* believe it. I know there are people in South Africa who desperately need help from someone like me."

With that, Joost shook his head, clenched his jaw, then impatiently raised his voice. "Lucas, you're talking nonsense. Things like that aren't changed by one person. It would be a fool's journey, doomed before it began!"

Lucas stared at the ground, then raised his fiery gaze to meet that of his uncle. "Something is leading me to go to Africa, even though I don't know what that 'something' is. I also don't yet know how I will get there, or what will happen to me when I do, but I do know . . . I must go."

Now realizing his argument was futile, Joost looked at the boy whose eyes he had once seen so joyous and full of life, and now instead seemed to be burning with a blaze that would not be extinguished.

The uncle shook his head and raised his hands in resignation. "All right, Lucas. You are of legal age, and you may do as you choose. As soon as we sell the house, I will give you whatever money comes from it, plus the sum your father left you. It will help you on your way."

He stood and motioned toward the inside of the house. "Come on, let's go in and get started . . ."

A week later, the house had been sold, and the new owners were ready to move into the fully furnished place. As far as Lucas's personal belongings were concerned, anything that could not be taken on an across-the-world journey was sold or donated.

As the uncle and nephew stood in front of the house on a nostalgic final visit approved by the new owners, Joost said kindly, "Lucas, here are your proceeds from the sale." He reached into his jacket pocket and pulled out a cashier's check made out to the young man for three thousand Dutch guilders. "It will help for a while, but you'll need to find work at some point in South Africa. I will stay here for another day or two in case I'm needed, and you can go ahead and get on your way. It's quite a long journey, as you know—and I will take you to the train station for your first leg of the trip. That would be Marseille, if I have researched your path correctly." He smiled.

Lucas reached out and accepted the check with an appreciative smile. "Yes, the train goes to Marseille, and from there I'll take a ship to South Africa. There are several stops in African countries along the way for restocking and refueling, but the trip should be complete in less than two weeks."

"What city will be your final destination, Lucas?"

Lucas looked at his uncle with a confidence that now made the older man feel as if this young Dutchman truly did have a destiny to be fulfilled on the dark continent.

"Cape Town."

Joost furrowed his brow and shook his head. "Lucas, it's all so . . . sudden. How will you get the travel documents you need?"

Lucas continued, unperturbed. "The train tickets are simple. As far as the ocean voyage, my father had a friend who was an executive at Union-Castle Line, so I reached out to him to help expedite the ticketing process for my passage from Marseille to Cape Town. I already have a passport that my parents obtained for me a year ago—they had planned on taking me abroad when I graduated . . ." His voice faded.

At that moment, a soft, cool breeze blew across the front sidewalk where the men were standing—a breeze that seemed to be ushering in a new life for young Lucas Van der Meer.

CHAPTER 5

When Lucas's uncle said goodbye outside the Amsterdam train station, the parting was bittersweet. In a way, Joost was terrified of what his nephew would be confronted with in Africa. In another way, he felt a twinge of envy—wishing *he* had done the same type of traveling at such a young age. He quietly admired not only Lucas's enthusiasm for this new adventure, but also the incredible courage that his nephew was displaying.

As Lucas started to walk away, he turned back and hugged Joost. "Thank you, Uncle Joost. I know my dad would be grateful for everything you have done, and I, too, am grateful. This journey is bigger than me, and I know there will be difficult times ahead. But I also know my faith is strong. I am prepared, and I won't let you or my parents down."

Now it was the older man who had tears welling up in his eyes. "Safe travels, Lucas. I know you will make a difference in Africa. If you ever need me, I will get there as fast as I possibly can. I love you."

With that, Lucas nodded and smiled, then picked up his lone suitcase and began the short walk toward the station entrance. Once inside, he exchanged his cashier's check for the currency he would need and walked the short distance to the ticket counter.

As the young traveler looked back toward where his uncle had been standing, his drifting thoughts were snapped back into the present as he heard the annoyed older clerk demanding, "Young man, did you hear me? The train is about to leave. You need to get on!"

Lucas nodded his understanding, paid for the ticket, then snatched up his luggage and dashed to join the other passengers onboard.

The trip south through Europe was pleasant, although it took a little longer than Lucas had hoped it would, even though he slept much of the way. With just a few short stops, the eighteen-hour journey took him through Holland, then into Belgium, and finally the train snaked its way through France down to its destination at Marseille.

Disembarking mid-morning from the train and then walking out into the French port area, Lucas's senses were overwhelmed. He smelled the salty, moist air, felt the warm, gentle sea breeze, and marveled at the lapping waves of crystal-clear blue water. The young Dutchman surveyed the surroundings, amazed by the sheer volume of cargo vessels and passenger ships in the distance. As he turned toward the town, the energy there seemed electrifying. People were scampering through the narrow, maze-like alleyways that connected the Mediterranean-style stone buildings with colorful shutters. Shopkeepers were opening their businesses, and vendors with carts of pastries, fruits, and vegetables lined the cobblestone streets.

Realizing his time before boarding the ship was short, Lucas spotted a small café about a hundred yards away, in between the train station and the area of the port where he would board the ship. He waded through the crowded street, teeming with people, cars, and bicycles, as he held his suitcase instinctively tighter until he reached his culinary destination.

Once he sat down, a waiter approached, and Lucas was able to use the bit of French he had learned in school to order eggs, cheese, a croissant, and a cup of coffee. When the food came, he scarfed it down, paid the server with a few francs he had gotten, and then continued briskly on to the next part of his journey.

Approaching the ship, his mind drifted. He thought about how the time between exiting the train, snagging a bite at the café, and then ending up at the footbridge to his boat at the port was a whirlwind—just like the weeks before he left Holland. He wondered when, if ever, his life would settle down again.

He didn't wonder long, however, as the next sound jolted him back to the present moment. It was the voice of a heavyset, short man booming "Ticket please!" in a deep French accent as Lucas reached the ticketing checkpoint at the top of the gangway. The gruff man reached out and took the paper that Lucas offered him, inspecting the document and then comparing it to the booking records. The crew member, wearing a crisply pressed white uniform, looked at Lucas and then smugly commented, "Not sure how you got *that* approved, but nevertheless, 2B is your cabin—up the stairs, to the left."

Lucas furrowed his brow at the curious reaction, but then he mumbled a curt "Merci," which the agent clearly was not interested in hearing. Shaking his head in annoyance, the man motioned for the young Dutchman to move on as the next passenger stepped up.

Lugging his suitcase, Lucas reached the top of the stairs, feeling the fatigue from his journey up to this point setting in. He turned and walked twenty steps to cabin 2B, placed his key in the lock, then smiled as the key turned smoothly and the door opened. Entering the room, he saw it was simple but well furnished. It seemed like a peaceful, welcome refuge as he reflected again on the boarding officer's curiously unwelcoming comment.

Putting that thought aside, Lucas began unpacking his suitcase to start the process of settling in for the final leg of his journey. He placed his few clothes in the drawer and then gently set the framed, small, black-and-white photograph of his parents on top of the dark cherry nightstand. Once he arranged it to his liking, he pulled back from the photo, but his gaze remained fixed on it as the memories began flooding in: the nights at the dinner table, the early morning walks with his father, the school activities his parents never missed. He still believed the journey he was embarking on was one he was destined to take, but with his nostalgic thoughts of home came the first fleeting doubt about his decision.

Lucas reached back down, picked up the photograph, and pulled it close to his heart as tears flowed down his cheeks.

A few moments later, Lucas made his way out to the deck to watch as the ship departed from the French harbor. With a blaring horn, the steamship pulled away while Lucas leaned on the iron rail, staring out at the sea. He was feeling so many emotions—he missed his parents with a depth of pain he didn't know he could feel, and yet he also had a deep feeling of contentment in his decision to go to Africa. He couldn't explain it. All those nights in his room reading about distant, exotic places seemed, oddly enough, to have been preparing him for this new world and the unknown mission ahead.

As the European mainland became progressively distant, his determination seemed to grow more resolute, although he also got the feeling he was not only leaving his homeland behind . . . but a part of his soul.

The ship sailed southwest into the Atlantic toward its first stop—Sierra Leone in West Africa—and Lucas walked around the deck to gain some familiarity with his new surroundings. There were plenty of people on board, and he seemed to be the youngest by far—but the only passenger "of color." He reflected on his uncle's words regarding the different races in South Africa. How *would* he be accepted? Would he meet others like himself?

After a bit more wandering, he drifted back over to the ship's railing. He felt the warm ocean air blowing in his face as he began to think back again on his Dutch home. He remembered the times his mother would cook for them and tell stories about the Egyptian household she grew up in, and how the meals had been served for hundreds of years with the same family recipe. She would share stories that seemed to be of another world—one that Lucas knew he also wanted to experience someday.

Just then, his thoughts were interrupted by a gentle voice coming from behind him. "Excuse me, may I stand here with you?"

Lucas's heart fluttered as he turned to see a young woman about his age with long, wavy blonde hair and bright, blue eyes, wearing a white lace dress that fit her perfectly.

"Er, um, of course," he stammered. Lucas felt flushed as she moved next to him, their arms propped side by side on the ship's railing. For a moment, they gazed out at the endless sea, then the woman broke the silence.

"I'm Victoria," she said with a smile, pulling back her windblown hair from her face.

"Lucas," he replied quickly.

"Where are you from, Lucas?"

The young man blushed. "Amsterdam."

Sizing him up, she giggled playfully. "Well, you're quite handsome, but I must say you don't look very Dutch to me."

He had become quite used to that observation from people he met. He explained, "My mum is—um, *was*—from Egypt and my father was from Holland. Guess the North African genes won out. Where are you from?"

She politely glossed over Lucas's use of the past tense to refer to his parents. "I'm from Cape Town. I've been in Europe visiting family with my mother, and now we are headed back home. As much as I enjoyed the snow, I must admit I'm ready for a little warm weather again."

Lucas laughed. "I could certainly use some of that also. We don't get a whole lot of warm weather this time of year where I'm from."

Victoria ran her fingers through her hair, gently pushing the wind-blown locks out of her eyes again as she gazed at Lucas. "It's interesting, isn't it? We always seem to want what we don't have. I would love to have the seasons change like they do in Holland. The weather in South Africa is either warm or dreadfully hot—nothing much else." She rolled her eyes playfully and smiled.

With a pensive expression, Lucas responded, "I suppose you're right. There have been many days I have wished for warm weather when it's freezing in Amsterdam. But overall, I would say it's a beautiful place to be. Well, it *was* a nice place to be . . ." His voice trailed off.

Victoria raised a curious eyebrow. "Why did you leave Amsterdam?"

He said thoughtfully, "I would say I wanted to make a change, and I believe—I mean, I *know*—that Africa is the place for me to make that change. Timing and faith are everything, and I think both of those are leading me there."

Not wanting to elaborate on his new, vulnerable feelings which he had not shared with anyone, Lucas changed the subject. "So, what about you? Just wanted to go visit family?"

Victoria looked down to gather her thoughts, and then back up at Lucas. "I suppose. Quite often while I was away, I wondered why I was *really* there. I went to visit my aunt and cousins, but I was hoping along the way I would also get some clarity as to . . . my next steps in life."

Just then, Lucas caught a glimpse of the large diamond ring on her finger.

"That's a beautiful ring you have on. Did *that* have anything to do with the clarity you were seeking?"

Victoria seemed surprised, as if Lucas had glimpsed into her soul in a way that no one had done in a long time—if ever. She shrugged nonchalantly. "Probably so. Eighteen is an age I guess a young woman could feel she has a right to be considered grown. But making grown decisions also leads to long-term or life-long consequences. I'm just not sure if I am ready to be grown—or married." She smiled.

Lucas nodded. "I understand. I've had to make some difficult, 'grown' decisions myself lately, including going on this trip. However, I think sometimes life pushes you in the direction you need to go."

The girl smiled. "My father said life would also put the right people in our personal world that we need to have at the right time." She paused and met Lucas with tender, kind eyes.

Lucas's nervous gaze fell to the deck as an emotion coursed through him that he could honestly say he had never experienced. He wasn't sure *what* it was, but Lucas did know he felt comforted—and that was exactly what he needed. "Yes, I agree with your father. I believe people and choices are put before us when we need them—if we would only pay attention."

Victoria's lips curled up into a smile, and again, Lucas felt himself blushing. Victoria seemed to notice because she politely dropped her gaze, and then looked at her watch. "Lucas, we've been here an hour! It's almost dinnertime, and my mother will be wondering where I am."

She extended her soft, white hand toward the young man. "It's very nice to meet you, Lucas. I know we will run into each other again on the ship. After all, it's quite a small vessel, and it will be a long journey."

Lucas nodded and shook her outreached hand gently. "Alright, I will look forward to that, Victoria. Thank you for talking with me."

Victoria smiled again, and when she turned away, Lucas couldn't help but notice her blonde hair glistening in the setting sun. He tried not to stare, but when she unexpectedly whirled around, she caught the young man stealing a fleeting, final glimpse. A broad grin came across Victoria's face as she turned to make her way back to her cabin.

Lucas decided to head back to his own quarters, and on the way, he thought about how much he had relished the conversation with Victoria, brief as it was. There was a connection between the two of them that Lucas couldn't deny, and he smiled at the thought of her.

Maybe on this trip, as Victoria had suggested, he would indeed meet the right people . . . at just the right time.

CHAPTER 6

The next few days came and went quickly on the ship, with Lucas managing to see Victoria only a few times. He would have loved to have seen her more, but she was typically with her mother. Something gave him the feeling that her mother had tight control over Victoria and whom she associated with, so he decided to keep his distance when he saw them together.

It didn't take long to realize he had made an excellent decision . . .

When the boat docked in the hot, humid, palm-laden Sierra Leone capital of Freetown for the first restocking, Lucas saw Victoria and her mother leaving the ship, most likely to do a little shopping and have some lunch. Lucas soon left the ship also, unsure of his surroundings, with this being his first visit to an African country. But after an hour of walking around a village near the dock and then grabbing a quick bite of lunch at a quaint French restaurant, he started to feel more comfortable. After the excellent meal and then another stroll down a street of local shops and vendor stands, he looked at his watch and realized the ship would again be departing soon. He wiped the perspiration from his brow and began the short walk back to the vessel before it left the harbor without him.

As he arrived on the deck of the boat, Lucas turned a corner and found himself face-to-face with Victoria, standing beside her mother.

The young South African girl glanced up at the tall, older woman, then turned to Lucas and offered nervously, "Oh, my! Hi, Lucas. I . . . would like you to meet my mother, Mrs. Lubbers."

Lucas awkwardly returned, "How do you do, ma'am?" as he extended his hand in greeting.

Ignoring the gesture, she turned on her heel to walk away, snapping, "Let's go, Victoria. The ship will be leaving soon." Glancing back toward Lucas, she added bitterly, "You're lucky this is a Union-Castle ship. If it were a South African vessel, you'd never be on this deck in the first place."

With that, an embarrassed Victoria had her wrist grabbed by her mother and was then quickly led away.

Lucas stood stunned and motionless, a sinking feeling in his stomach. As the two women walked into the distance, Lucas could hear them arguing intensely and he saw Victoria jerk away from her mother's grasp. Dejected at the feeling he had been the cause of their disagreement, Lucas went back to his cabin and prepared for a night's rest. After turning off the light, he lay on the bed and put the soft pillow over his head, trying unsuccessfully to escape the heavy waves of embarrassment that were still rolling through him . . .

The next morning, Lucas woke with nagging questions about the interaction he had on the deck with Victoria's mother the evening before. Was this another example of the attitude his Uncle Joost said he would experience in South Africa? Lucas's heart sank, but he was determined to push through any challenge he faced, and he decided this would simply be one of his first to overcome.

He also decided it was in his and Victoria's best interests to steer clear of each other for the rest of the trip. If Mrs. Lubbers did not want her daughter near him, he had to honor that, much to his chagrin. But even though he couldn't see her, there was something about Victoria that Lucas just could not—and *would not*—stop thinking about . . .

The ship briefly pulled into port at two more countries, Liberia and Ghana, as the journey down the African coast continued. Each time, Lucas chose to remain on board, not wanting to risk running into Victoria and her mother. He tried to justify his decision by telling himself there was nothing he wanted to see in those places, anyway. *It's time to get focused on the*

business at hand in South Africa—whatever that business will be, he reminded himself.

Just before the boat docked in Cape Town, Lucas had packed all his belongings into his suitcase, and he decided to go onto the deck for a last bit of ocean air and maritime scenery.

As fate would have it, when he walked out to the part of the ship where he had met Victoria the first time . . . there she was again. His heart began beating faster until he felt it would jump out of his chest. Victoria's eyes widened in excitement as she turned and saw him. "There you are, Lucas! I've looked all over for you for the last week—where have you been hiding?"

Lucas mumbled, "Well, yes, *hiding* is probably the appropriate word. I didn't think your mum would approve . . ."

Victoria's tender expression said everything. "Lucas, I'm sorry. My parents' views are different from mine—much different. In my opinion, their perspectives are barbaric, cruel, and . . . unforgivable. I am so sorry. I just don't know what to say except, thank you for not judging me to be like my mother. She and I are nothing alike, and this trip showed me that more than ever."

Victoria reached out, took the young man's hands, and pleaded, "Do you believe me?"

Her soft hands felt like those of a princess, and Lucas smiled. He *did* believe her—with everything in his being. The way she compassionately spoke reminded him so much of his mother's unconditional kindness. Without hesitation, he exclaimed, "Yes, of course, Victoria! Thank you for telling me that. I had hoped that was the way you felt."

She smiled broadly. "Lucas, you have helped me feel something I haven't felt in years. You also affirmed to me that people are people—no matter what my parents have told me to the contrary. We are all the same. I also know now that the man I am engaged to does not have the ability to make me feel the way I felt in the conversations you and I had."

With his hands still cradled in hers, Lucas felt tears of joy welling up in his eyes. "Victoria, I . . ."

Just then, their conversation was interrupted as the pair heard a shout from behind them. "Victoria, get his filthy hands away from you and come over here right this moment! What did I tell you? He is not your type, and he is not even your race—you will have nothing to do with him. Do you hear me—get over here!" With that, Victoria's mother grabbed her daughter by the shoulder and pulled her away from Lucas. "Go pack your suitcase immediately, Victoria. The ship will dock in twenty minutes, and we will be the first ones off, or you will regret it. Am I clear?"

The young woman bristled. "Yes, Mother Dear. There are *many* things I already regret . . ."

At that comment, Victoria was again forcefully taken away, but not before she said softly, "I am sorry, Lucas.

I am so sorry. I wish you every good thing imaginable in Cape Town, and I am so grateful I met you. Maybe someday, somehow . . ." Her voice trailed off.

Lucas's heart sank as he stared at Victoria being led away. Her mother's eyes bored into Lucas with contempt as she hissed, "If you ever go near my daughter again, it will be the last thing you do."

Right then, with the ship steaming slowly into the Cape Town port, Lucas felt a chill up his spine as he made out the words on the large sign hovering over the dock—words which now seemed to be issuing a dire warning to him:

WELCOME TO SOUTH AFRICA

CHAPTER 7

As the ship docked in Cape Town, it occurred to Lucas that he was not only on a different continent but also that the seasons were opposite from those in Europe. It was approaching spring in the northern hemisphere when he had left, but in South Africa, today was a bright, warm fall day.

As the passengers disembarked, Lucas was near the back of the line. He stood on his toes to get above the crowd, and then he squinted anxiously into the sun, searching for Victoria. When he finally spotted her, he saw the two women were among the first passengers to leave the ship—just as her mother had demanded. As they walked off, Victoria turned, scouring the crowd for Lucas. When their eyes met, it felt *magical* to the young man. Even at a distance, it seemed as though he was gazing into the eyes of a woman who had in a short period of time made him the happiest man in the world.

But then, he felt a queasiness in his stomach, sensing he would never see her again.

Victoria waved goodbye as subtly as she could, hoping to evade her mother's line of sight. Unfortunately, the matronly woman caught a glimpse of Lucas waving in return. As before, she abruptly pulled her daughter away, and then as they quickly entered the building to begin the South African customs process, the pair disappeared from Lucas's sight.

Strangely, even though Lucas's time with Victoria had been brief, he now felt all alone. Holding his suitcase tightly, he pondered his next move in this new land as the line inched forward toward the old, gray building.

Reaching the front of the deboarding line where he had lost sight of Victoria, Lucas saw two doors. Without hesitation, he moved toward the opening Victoria and her mother had entered through. Lucas, however, was then met by a husky, grim South African policeman who held up both hands to stop the young man from moving forward.

"Wrong door," he uttered firmly.

Lucas looked up quickly and saw the sign: WHITES ONLY. He suddenly felt confused and panicked.

The officer sternly put his hands on Lucas's shoulders and turned him until he was facing the door to his left, labeled COLOUREDS, next to another entrance with a sign that read BLACKS.

The reality then sank in as to where his place would be in the eyes of this country.

He stepped meekly to the next door and entered the short queue, waiting for his turn to be processed. Lucas took in the dirty surroundings and the antiquated furniture and equipment in the area. Then he peered out the door and across the way, spotting the clean, well-maintained area for the privileged ones.

The young Dutchman felt his pulse racing as he realized nothing in his travel books had prepared him for *this*. Lucas shuffled forward, and as the line moved, he was acutely aware of the queasy feeling in the pit of his stomach.

When he reached the front of the line, the worker took Lucas's papers and scrutinized them carefully. He then handed the young man a small booklet, stamped with a designation that would keep Lucas away from any area that was off-limits to his race. "Here is your *dompas*," the man said matter-of-factly, as he handed him a small passbook.

Lucas squinched up his face as he scanned it.

"You must keep it with you wherever you go, and always be willing to show it when asked by those who are in authority over you."

Lucas nodded his understanding, put the *dompas* in the inside pocket of his green field jacket, and walked through the crowds into the hallway which led outside. When he stepped out, he saw what appeared to be tens of thousands of people bustling around. In all the confusion, he began scanning the area for a bus to take him to a hotel—even though he had no idea where he was going to go.

A police officer quickly walked over and reprimanded him. "Please get in the correct line."

Realizing he was once again in the wrong place, Lucas lifted his gaze up and around to find the sign stating COLOUREDS. When he reached the door of the bus, his eyes met those of the driver, and Lucas asked nervously where he could find a hotel for the night. The brown-skinned employee commented neutrally, "Get on—the hotel is less than half an hour away."

The young man obliged, climbing the steps onto the overcrowded bus then marching down the narrow aisle, finally squeezing into a middle seat in the last row. He noticed once again that the bus was not clean, and it seemed in poor condition. Even though gasoline-powered vehicles had been in this part of South Africa for ten years or so, this bus was already exceptionally worn. He looked out the window and saw the shiny, modern buses the "other" passengers were boarding.

The entire scenario seemed not only incredibly illogical and strange, but now it was making Lucas . . . *angry and resentful.* Less than a month ago, he was living in a beautiful home in Amsterdam, and his mother and father were highly respected citizens in their community. Lucas had plenty of friends, and he had no wants or needs. Now, in the blink of an eye, he was in another world—one where it seemed he was not welcome, simply because of his brown skin, which he had been so proud of due to his mother's Egyptian heritage.

It's not right, he furiously thought. Down deep, Lucas knew he wanted to fight to change this—yet now he wondered . . . *how?* But at this point, he was so exhausted that he didn't feel like fighting anything—he just wanted to sleep.

As the twenty-minute trip to the hotel began, it was soon clear which parts of the city Lucas would be welcome in, and in the distance, he saw which parts of the city he would not dare set foot in. As the bus continued its course, it became increasingly obvious to Lucas he was in a country now where the rule-makers had the same horrible, twisted philosophy as Victoria's mother.

Just then, Lucas's thoughts were jolted back to the present as the bus pulled up to a stop at an aging, red-brick hotel in a rundown part of town. "District Six, here you go, young man," the bus driver yelled out, glancing in his mirror toward the back of the bus.

Lucas stood and peered warily out the window at the hotel, and then started moving toward the door of the bus. Once he got to the front, he reached into his pocket, pulled out a few shillings, and handed them to the driver, who calmly offered, "Good luck."

Lucas nodded and stepped off the bus, and as it pulled away, he found himself staring up at a faded wooden sign that read THE COOPER HOTEL. The place wasn't anything like he would have expected a week ago, but now Lucas's expectations had dramatically changed. As he approached the glass front door, three beggars in tattered clothes appeared from different directions, pleading for money. Lucas didn't know what to do, so he simply pushed them away and hurried inside the building.

The elderly, dark-skinned man at the reception desk scrutinized Lucas through horn-rimmed glasses. With a deep South African accent, he asked in a decidedly unfriendly tone, "How may I help you?"

Still overwhelmed by his surroundings, the young man replied faintly, "I would like a room." Then he hesitated and finally added, "For two nights please." *Yes*, he thought, *that should give me enough time to collect my wits and put together a plan.* That was what he needed—a plan of any kind, at this point.

The older gentleman thumbed through a ragged notebook in front of him until he found the page he needed. He ran his eyes to the bottom, put his index finger on the last line, and replied without enthusiasm, "Yes, I have one room left for two nights. That will be ten shillings. Please pay now." The clerk held out his hand toward the young man.

Lucas reached into his jacket pocket again, retrieved the necessary money, and put it in the man's outstretched palm as the clerk then took it and gave Lucas a large brass key. "Room 220. Up the stairs, turn right, and it's the second room on the right. Please don't make noise at night as we have other guests in the hotel."

Lucas nodded in agreement, picked up his suitcase, and walked up the short flight of stairs. When he reached the hallway, it was dark and outdated, with the light green-and-orange paint peeling off the walls. He walked a few steps over to room 220, put the large key in the keyhole, turned it, and then opened the loudly creaking door. Surveying the room, he saw, like the rest of the hotel, it was old and dated, but nevertheless, it was a place to stay. He entered and set his suitcase down by the single bed, walked over to the window, and pulled back the curtains. The street and surrounding areas had little activity, and there appeared to be a distinct lack of happiness as the people seemed to have no interest in connecting with each other. Across the road was a row of vacant storefronts, and all six spaces looked as if they had not been occupied in years.

Moving his face closer to the glass, Lucas took in a lengthy view of the street. There were a few random shops in the distance that appeared to be open, but overall, the landscape was dismal. He also noticed that unlike the privileged areas they had passed on the bus ride, there were few cars here. Pedestrians, people on bicycles, and workers pulling carts dotted the street, but it was as if modernization was not being allowed to happen in this part of the community. Like the ones who had approached him earlier, he saw more beggars, simply trying to survive in the harsh surroundings. Now that Lucas had his wits about him, he wished he had given the poor solicitors some money. He shook his head and pulled the curtains shut to block out the entire depressing scene.

He walked across the room on the worn, green carpet, turned on a small lamp, and sat on his bed. "*Where am I?*" he bemoaned.

Placing his head in his hands, Lucas now tried desperately to make sense of what had happened over the last month. First, he had lost his parents, then his home. Now he had come on this journey to make a positive difference in the country, and he was suddenly wrestling with the terrifying question, *How could I possibly affect change here?* The fearful, cluttering thoughts began to cascade uncontrollably through his mind. *What have I done? Maybe Uncle Joost was right, and I should go to Geneva after all. Would I even be able to go back? What about the money that will soon begin to dwindle?*

Fighting back tears and now feeling as if he was physically and mentally approaching his breaking point, Lucas stretched out on the bed, feebly turned his gaze to the ceiling, and prayed fervently and desperately for God to send him a sign that he was on the right course.

At that moment, every tense muscle in the tormented young Dutchman's body seemed to relax in unison, and Lucas Van der Meer immediately fell into a deep, long-overdue sleep . . .

CHAPTER 8

When Lucas awoke the next morning, he found himself lying in the same position he had fallen asleep in.

Sitting up slowly, he ran his fingers through his dark hair, shook his head, and rubbed his eyes. Hoping to wake himself up a bit, Lucas pulled back the covers, stepped out of bed, and walked over to the window to pull the shade up and let some sunlight in. It was 7:30, so the Cape Town sun was fully risen as Lucas watched the trickling stream of activity on the street.

He turned back toward the room, but then did a double take. Across the street, he saw the same empty storefronts—except for one. Directly across from his room, above the window of the now seemingly occupied shop, was a metal sign with beige letters that read SHOE REPAIR. Lucas cocked his head in curiosity. *That was not there yesterday,* he thought to himself. However, the "new" store appeared well established.

Deeply curious, Lucas decided to investigate. He took a fast shower, threw on a pair of jeans and a faded green T-shirt, then slipped on some old brown loafers and headed out of his room toward the cobbler shop.

The young man reached the lobby of the hotel and there was the same grumpy employee from the day before at the front desk. "Excuse me, sir," Lucas asked hesitantly. "The shoe repair shop . . . has it been across the street for long?"

The attendant seemed bothered and didn't even look up at the young man. "Don't know. I don't pay attention to those things."

Lucas shook his head and pursed his lips, annoyed at the answer. *Never mind*, he thought, *I'll find out for myself.* He turned and walked down the short hallway to the front door and pushed it open, immediately feeling the heat of the South African morning. He stepped into the street, dodging a few bicycles and unconcerned pedestrians as he crossed.

When he reached the other side, he walked over the cracked sidewalk and stepped up to the front door of the little shop. Turning the knob and then pulling the door open cautiously, he immediately took in the familiar fragrance of new leather as he entered the business. He noticed small handwritten signs throughout the store, along with a wide selection of shoes the cobbler had apparently made or repaired.

Behind the counter, a short, medium-built gentleman with chocolate-brown skin stood reading to himself from a tattered piece of paper. Noting the man's tight, gray afro, Lucas surmised he was in his seventies.

Carefully folding the paper and putting it in his shirt pocket, the man then raised his eyes and offered his visitor a smile. "Good morning, Lucas."

Furrowing his brow, the young man stammered, "Excuse me?"

The shopkeeper cocked his head in mock surprise as he repeated cheerfully, "Good morning, Lucas!"

Still flustered, the Dutchman replied, "Sir, um, how do you know my name? Have we met?"

The cobbler walked a few steps closer. He grinned and said with a twinkle in his eyes, "Well, we've met *now*. As far as knowing your name, you *look* like a Lucas."

Lucas smiled and shook his head, perceiving the gentleman was harmless—and kind. "Really? What exactly does a 'Lucas' look like?"

The man shrugged. "Well, I suppose a Lucas would look exactly like . . . you." He laughed.

Lucas couldn't help but grin, although he was still perplexed. "So, I'm guessing we *have* met somewhere, or someone let you know I was here. Probably has something to do with me traveling with that stupid donkey pass."

The cobbler belly laughed. "Oh, that old thing. Well, it's a little bit annoying, but you'll get used to it. I think the proper term is *dompas*."

Lucas felt himself blushing. "Oh, right, sorry," he said with a nervous smile.

The cobbler reached out his hand in greeting as his lips curled up into a smile. "I am Eli, at your service. 'The Cobbler of Cape Town,' some would call me."

"Lucas Van der Meer," the young man replied, shaking the outstretched hand firmly.

"Well, Lucas, did you come in for a shoeshine, a shoe repair, or what?"

"None of those, I'm afraid, although I am sure I will need your service someday. I really wanted to ask you, 'How long has your shop been here?' I could have sworn it wasn't in this spot yesterday when I checked into the hotel across the street."

Eli looked around Lucas and squinted toward the hotel. "Ah, yes, that's a nice little place," he jested, clearly avoiding the question.

Lucas shook his head in disagreement. "It's mediocre, I would say, but beggars can't be choosers, I suppose. Now about your store. It seems it just . . . appeared overnight."

Eli smiled and rubbed his chin again. "Change can happen quickly—can't it, Lucas?"

There was something about the cobbler's question that seemed odd. Did he know about the change in Lucas's life that happened so suddenly? Was he just making conversation? Lucas furrowed his brow, then chose to respond to the cobbler's question.

"Yes, Eli, change can happen in a heartbeat—whether we are ready for it, or not."

Eli nodded. "I do understand that. I lost my father when I was fifteen. I was certainly not ready—but then again, I don't know if I would have *ever* been ready."

Suddenly, Lucas felt kindred of spirit with this mysterious, gentle man. "I'm very sorry. Was he a cobbler also?"

Eli managed a smile as he gazed into the distance, clearly lost in thought. "Yes, he was one of the best cobblers in all of Africa. He taught me so much, and I am eternally grateful."

Lucas nodded empathetically. "My father was a university professor—also one of the best in the country at what he did. He taught me unselfishly about learning . . . and about life."

Eli smiled. "An excellent mentor can provide us with invaluable insight and wisdom."

Lucas paused. "I agree. I miss my mentors more than I can say."

The cobbler leaned forward on the counter, listening intently as Lucas decided to share his plight. "My mother and father died earlier this month. They were the most important people in my life, and I feel lost without them. I came to Africa because I always told my parents I wanted to make a difference in the world. For some reason I felt I was led here."

"Do you still feel that way?" Eli followed up with a raised eyebrow.

Lucas shrugged his shoulders. "I still feel like this is where I need to be, but I'll admit I had no idea it was going to be this difficult. It's like I am still trying to figure out everything—or anything—in this new world. Honestly, I feel so . . . alone."

Eli nodded. "I understand. Sometimes it feels as if I am on my own, and I just don't have a clue as to what I am doing. But I always figure it out, and so will you, my friend."

Lucas managed a smile. "Eli, I must admit, I was praying last night that I would receive a sign that I am doing the right thing by being here in Africa. I'm already starting to believe that maybe *you* are that sign . . ."

Eli grinned knowingly. "We often don't know why we are put in the positions we are put in. But . . . if our faith is strong enough, and we are patient enough, the way will be made clear every time. I believe you are where you need to be, and you are going to make a difference in many lives. Trust me on that."

Lucas nodded his approval. "I can't tell you how much I needed to hear those words."

Then the young man brought the conversation back around. "But Eli, the shop . . . it really is new, right?"

Eli's eyes twinkled. "Oh, I guess you could say that. Then again, I've always been here—maybe you just couldn't see me."

Lucas scratched his head in confusion. "Wait. That's impossible."

Eli shrugged, and a sly smile appeared on his face. "I beg to differ. In my opinion, *impossible* is just a label—and I've never been one for labels."

Before Lucas could respond, the door swung open, and a petite, older African woman walked in with two pairs of worn shoes in her hands.

Arching her eyebrow, she asked Eli, "Are you the cobbler?"

"Well, I like to think so." He smiled as his pun seemed to put her at ease.

"My mother passed away last week. I have her funeral to attend, and my shoes—and my daughter's shoes—are in terrible shape. Unfortunately, they are the only suitable ones we have. Can you do anything about them? I . . . can't afford to buy new ones."

Eli took the shoes from the woman and set them on the counter, noting the collapsed heel and torn strap on each.

"Sometimes the most broken things just need some loving care to be brought back to their former glory."

The woman looked curiously at Eli as he added with a compassionate smile, "I believe that these shoes will be as good as new when I finish with them, and I think that you and your daughter will be quite pleased." He nodded and pointed to the footwear. "Give me a day, and I will have them ready for you—don't worry at all."

As Eli jotted down her name and contact information, the woman seemed to stand a little taller, as though the weight of the world had been taken off her. "I don't know anyone in Cape Town. I am from Durban, and my daughter and I just came into town for my mother's service, and I saw your sign. You are the first person I've met, and somehow you have already made me feel comforted. Thank you."

With that, the cobbler reached out to clasp the woman's hand, smiling. "It is an honor to meet you. I will see you when you return, ma'am, and here is my card if you have any questions at all." With that, Eli took a business card off the counter and handed it to her. The words "Eli Tambo, The Cobbler of Cape Town" were blazed across the card, and there was a small empty space at the bottom, where he had handwritten, "*I care, my friend.*"

The woman took the card, smiled, then turned and walked out the door.

Lucas was touched and impressed. "Eli, it was as if you had known that woman her whole life. I have never seen someone have a rapport like that with a stranger. It was . . . beautiful."

The man smiled gently and shook his head. "I am simply a cobbler, Lucas. I am pleased to make other people happy with my work. But it all starts when I genuinely let the customers know I am happy with *them*."

Lucas lifted an eyebrow. "What do you mean?"

The cobbler glanced at his watch. "We can talk more about this later. Come back tomorrow, and we will have breakfast. How about seven thirty?"

Lucas smiled. "I would love that. Where shall we meet?"

Eli turned toward the back, and with a sweeping gesture, offered, "How about here? I'll bring us something to eat. I have a little area where we can sit, and I make good South African breakfasts. It might not be the same level as your mother's cooking, but I'm sure you wouldn't mind starting off the day with a full belly." He laughed.

Lucas grinned and shook his head. "My mum used to say I could eat more than any human she had ever seen. I'll try to control myself for you—and I'll look forward to our time together."

Eli shrugged his shoulders and smiled. "Well, then, it's a date. I'll see you tomorrow, my friend."

Friend. Lucas liked the sound of that. He smiled, nodded, then turned and walked out the door to spend a day in Cape Town, seeing what his new homeland had to offer.

Little did he know, it would have more to offer than he could have ever dreamed . . .

CHAPTER 9

Lucas turned left out of the shop and began walking up the street, without any idea where he should be going. It didn't particularly matter because anywhere he went would be new to him at this point. He stepped into a few stores, always aware of the fact that people "like him" were the only ones he saw on his tour.

He still hadn't come to terms with the fact that a government could offer no need for an explanation of their belief that some people deserved less than others, simply because of their skin color. He thought about his parents and how neither of them would have accepted it—but the question Lucas was struggling with was, *What exactly would they have done about it?*

After an hour in the hot Cape Town sun, Lucas decided he had walked enough, so he hailed a taxi and asked the driver to show him around the city for the day. The tall, muscular, African man named Arthur was happy to do so, and after Lucas climbed in the back, the cabbie began by taking him to places that were significant because of the strong Dutch influence. It was all interesting to Lucas, even though he was embarrassed by what the early Hollanders had done all those years to the Cape Town native inhabitants. The irony wasn't lost on Lucas that even though he was from the Netherlands—as were the pioneers called the Trekkers—he felt like a prisoner in the same land the Dutch were so proud to have settled.

Just then, the cab driver pointed to a natural landmark becoming visible in the distance. "Table Mountain," he said excitedly. "It's one of the most famous points in all of Cape Town."

Lucas marveled at how the giant structure did indeed resemble the shape of a massive table. Then there was a quick drive to Camps Bay Beach—a beautiful, tranquil seaside area.

"Of course, you'll need to stay on the right side of the beach, my friend," the taxi driver said, shaking his head with a grim look.

Lucas saw the signs denoting which side of the beach people were allowed on, depending on their ethnicity, while Arthur watched the young man's disappointed reaction in his rearview mirror. The driver commented adamantly, "I don't know what it's going to take for things to change here—but they will change. Trust me, when the right person comes along, it *will* happen."

Lucas leaned back and took in those words. *Yes*, he thought, *someone will make it change. But . . . who would that be?*

The cab continued its slow, steady course throughout the different sections of Cape Town. But then, without warning, the driver stopped abruptly and let out a loud, steady stream of curse words.

"What happened?" Lucas yelled.

"I took a wrong turn," he shot back in an anxious voice. "We should not be here!"

In a panicked state, Arthur tried to quickly turn the cab around when suddenly, a large South African police officer appeared. The man stood menacingly in front of the car, his baton in hand, which he was tapping into his other palm.

He then walked arrogantly around to the driver's side, and Arthur slowly rolled down the window.

"*Dompas*, please," the officer said in an impatient tone.

Both men reached into their jackets and pulled out the required booklets, which the officer took.

The constable glanced at the documents and began incoherently shouting at the men. He then raised the club as if to strike Arthur, upon which Lucas cried compassionately, "No!"

Surprised, the officer stopped his club in mid-air and stared angrily at Lucas. Neither of the two terrified passengers knew what would happen next, but then the enraged man changed the course of his swing and brought the weapon down on the windshield of the vehicle, cracking the glass.

The cab driver at this point had put his hands up in front of his face to protect himself. When he pulled them down, he saw the exasperated officer turn and stomp away, upon which the cabbie hastily drove from the scene.

"Thank you, my friend. I am sorry," the still shaking Arthur said to Lucas.

The Dutchman reached up and put his hands on the driver's shoulder in a consoling gesture. "No, *I* am sorry. I clearly had no idea what life was like here. Plus, your cab . . . I feel terrible about this damage."

Arthur shook his head and continued to drive. Under his breath, this time in an angry tone, he repeated, "Someone will do something about this—someday . . ."

Lucas Van der Meer stared out the open window and felt the breeze on his face as the car sped away. "Yes," he echoed aloud in a firm tone. "Somebody will do something about this—and maybe sooner rather than later."

When the cab was near the hotel, Lucas smiled as he politely tried to lighten the mood. "That's probably enough excitement for the day—let's cut the tour a bit short, Arthur. You can go ahead and drop me off."

Appearing relieved, the cabbie nodded, and a minute later he pulled the vehicle up to the Cooper Hotel. Lucas stepped out and walked around to the driver's side, and as Arthur rolled down the window, Lucas slipped him the fare plus a generous tip.

"Thank you so much. I'm grateful," the cabbie replied humbly as he reached out and accepted the money.

"Hopefully that will help with the repairs—thank you again for taking me today," Lucas offered.

Arthur nodded. "It is more than generous." With that, he rolled up his window and then pulled out slowly into the early evening traffic.

As the cab faded into the distance, Lucas suddenly realized how hungry he was from the day's events. He turned and walked up the steps into the hotel, then went over to the front desk clerk and asked where the onsite restaurant was. The man stood, leaned over the desk, and then pointed to the end of the hall. Lucas uttered a quick "thank you" and headed down the corridor.

Reaching the restaurant, he noticed there were only a few patrons in the small, dimly lit place. "Sit wherever you'd like," the middle-aged hostess offered cheerfully. The young man plopped down at the nearest table, and immediately, a waiter of about the same age as Lucas walked up and handed him a menu.

"What's your suggestion?" Lucas asked with a smile.

"Ah, sir, you can't go wrong with the fried shark—probably the best in the city," the slim, tall worker replied.

Lucas's nervous look didn't go unnoticed by the server, who grinned and offered, "Trust me, sir. If you don't like it, I'll bring you something else."

"Deal," Lucas agreed. The young man took the menu and disappeared into the kitchen to present the order to the chef.

Lucas glimpsed a Cape Town newspaper in the chair beside him. Picking it up, he began to read about the events in the area and realized quickly that the newspaper was targeted at residents who were *non-Caucasian*. The articles were shallow, uninformative, and subjective. It was another reminder that the full story about pretty much *everything* was being withheld from residents in that part of Cape Town.

Lucas sipped his water, and his thoughts went back to the morning. *The time with Eli seemed so . . . synchronistic. Where did this man—and his cobbler's shop—come from, and how did he know who I was? Also, how did we have such a powerful rapport so quickly?*

Then he thought about the woman who entered the shop. *Was it coincidence that she ended up there? It was almost as if the shop attracted a person who needed to be there. But no, that's ridiculous . . . isn't it?*

His mind drifted back to Victoria sharing her father's wisdom about people arriving at the right time to teach the lessons that each person needs to receive. *Was Eli and his store providing that for people? Could that really be possible?*

Lucas's thoughts were interrupted when the waiter showed up with the hungry young man's meal. Surprisingly, it looked rather tasty—although people in Amsterdam would have thought he was crazy if he told them he was dining on . . . *shark.*

He grinned to himself and then took a small bite. *Not bad,* he thought.

In just a few moments, Lucas had finished the entire meal. When the waiter approached, he saw the cleaned plate and laughed. "Wow, it must have been pretty decent, eh?"

"I never would have expected it," Lucas said, laughing along with the man. "We don't have a lot of sharks in Holland."

The waiter cocked his head and raised a curious eyebrow. "Holland? Really? I've always wondered what life is like in Europe. Are you from there?"

Lucas chuckled. "I think I need to get a sign to carry around with me that says, 'Yes, I really am from Holland.' My mother was from Egypt, so . . ."

The waiter shook his head and began backstepping his words. "I am so sorry, I didn't . . ."

Lucas held up his hand to stop him. "No offense taken. I was just teasing. By the way, what's your name?"

The young man let out a sigh of relief. "Joseph. And yours?"

"I'm Lucas. It's very nice to meet you." Without thinking, he then blurted out, "You were asking about Europe. Have you ever been there?"

Joseph threw his head back and laughed. "Sir, it would be . . . impossible."

Realizing the unrealistic nature of the question, now it was Lucas's turn to backtrack. "Forgive me. I didn't think about the policies here. I still have not adjusted to the laws the government has imposed on the citizens—except for the 'chosen ones,' I guess."

"I suppose that's a good way to put it, Lucas. From what I understand, it's the way it has always been, and the way it will always be—but maybe even worse days are coming."

Lucas cocked his head and asked, "What do you mean?"

"The laws which restrict us are increasing. They restrict our movements, our rights to own property, our ability to have good jobs . . ." He shook his head.

"It's just unthinkable," Lucas said incredulously.

"Yes," the waiter answered back. "Yet, this is *reality*—for all of us."

Lucas stared blankly at the waiter, realizing the young man was right—it was now *his* reality, too.

After a little more conversation, Lucas asked for the check.

"Here you go, sir," Joseph said, handing him the bill.

Lucas chuckled. "Oh, I am definitely not a *sir* . . . but I *would* like to be your friend."

Joseph shook Lucas's now outstretched hand and smiled. "I would like that too, Lucas. It's nice to meet you, and I am sure I'll be seeing you around."

Lucas nodded in agreement, handed Joseph enough cash to cover the meal and a hefty tip, then pushed back from the table and headed upstairs to turn in early for the night.

Even though he didn't know it at the time, tomorrow was going to be the first of many extraordinary days ahead . . .

CHAPTER 10

Lucas awoke refreshed, and when he remembered he had an appointment with the Cobbler of Cape Town, he was excited. He couldn't wait to learn more about this mysterious man, and he couldn't help but now believe Eli had come into his life for a reason.

Looking at his watch, Lucas saw he had thirty minutes to get ready, so he jumped in the shower and completed his morning ritual quickly. Once he walked out the door of the hotel, he curiously noted that the street activity was busier than in the last two days. He also saw the cobbler's shop wasn't quite open yet, evidenced by the CLOSED sign still displayed.

Walking up to the shop doorstep, Lucas put his nose up to the glass on the door, but then seemingly out of nowhere, Eli appeared and opened it. "Come in, my friend. I made some muffins and fresh coffee for us."

Lucas grinned as he entered the business. "Sounds great, Eli. Do you live close by?"

The cobbler pointed to an old but well cared-for bike propped near the front counter. "Only about a ten-minute ride to get here, depending on how fast these legs are peddling." He chuckled and motioned for Lucas to join him at the back of the shop.

Lucas nodded and followed close behind, taking in the surroundings along the way. "It's all so organized!"

Eli smiled. "I have to keep it that way—otherwise I wouldn't be able to find a shoe to save my life!"

Once they reached the back room, the older gentleman pointed to a small table. "Have a seat, your server will be right out."

Lucas was puzzled, but then Eli followed up with a grin, "Well, he'll look just like me."

As Lucas sat down, the cobbler stepped over to another small table where he had placed a picnic basket and a pot of coffee. Reaching into the basket, he pulled out and then carefully unfolded a soft red-and-white checkered cloth, revealing two muffins, which he placed on small plates and carried to the main table. He then poured two cups of coffee, setting one in front of Lucas and taking the other for himself.

"Please, try out my handiwork," Eli said as he gestured toward the delicacy on Lucas's plate.

Lucas picked up the muffin and eagerly took a bite. "Apple! My favorite!"

Somehow already aware of that, the cobbler raised an eyebrow calmly and tilted his head. "Is that so?"

Lucas shook his head and teased, "Eli, I have to say, I haven't gotten you figured out yet."

"Well, it's okay. Sometimes I think I haven't gotten me figured out yet either." The cobbler chuckled.

The young man smiled and then started to speak, but then he stopped.

Noting the hesitation, Eli cocked his head and wondered aloud, "Thinking about something?"

Lucas nodded. "Eli, I am thinking about a lot of things. I am thinking about how I ended up in South Africa, how I ended up meeting you, how I . . ."

Eli held up his hand to stop him. "So, let me ask you this . . . if you knew the answers to those questions, would it change anything about your current situation?"

"Well, no, I suppose not."

"So then, it seems to me, the best thing to think about is, 'What shall I do with the current situation I am in? How will I use my life at this point to impact the world?'"

Lucas looked puzzled, which led Eli to continue. "As I told you, I lost my father when I was fifteen, so you and I, at minimum, have *that* in common. But I think there's much more . . ."

The young man nodded slowly and began listening carefully.

"I did not know my life would take the course it has taken. I would not have chosen some of the things that have happened to me. But what I *would* choose is the chance I have had to change people's lives. That is what I am doing with the gift God has given me. I believe you are going to do the same thing."

Lucas sounded encouraged as he said, "You really believe that?"

"With every ounce of my being. I also believe that you and I can do this together."

Lucas rubbed his chin. "You mean, *work* together?"

Eli nodded firmly. "Yes. But I also mean change the world together."

The room became quiet as Lucas tried to absorb the words he had just heard.

"*Change . . . the world?*" he rasped.

Eli calmly took a bite of his muffin and then took a sip of coffee. After a few seconds, he gently replied, "Yes, starting with this community that desperately needs it."

Lucas was speechless as he stared at the cobbler, who continued, "Remember when I said not to focus on the past?"

Lucas nodded.

"Remember when I also said 'impossible' is simply a label—which I'm not a big fan of?"

Lucas swallowed and nodded again.

"You are here for a reason, Lucas. The shop opens in ten minutes. I would like you to stay here today and simply observe. At the end of the day, you can tell me if you would like to join me on my mission. If not, you may go your own way, with no hard feelings. On the other hand, if you choose to accept my offer, we will change the city, which will at some point change the country, which will eventually change the world. We will do it together—one person at a time. I don't know exactly how, but I know it will be done."

Lucas's throat tightened. "Eli, I know what you said about the label 'impossible,' but, do you honestly believe this can happen?"

The older man replied slowly and evenly, "Everything is possible for those who believe, Lucas. *Everything*."

As if they had just had a simple conversation about the weather, Eli smiled, stood up, and then gestured with his coffee cup toward Lucas's meal. "Enjoy your breakfast. I'll get the shop ready to open, and you may join me whenever you choose." He gently pushed the chair back into place and then disappeared into the front of the store.

Lucas's head was spinning. It all sounded unbelievable, but at the same time, it seemed like he was *meant* to do it. Maybe he had been preparing for this place all his life. The skills he had learned from his parents, the love he had for people, the books he had read about Africa, the mental strength he had been forced to develop after the accident . . . now it all seemed to be pointing him to doing this—whatever *this* was.

Lucas finished his muffin, downed his coffee, returned the dishes to the picnic basket, and then went to find Eli.

Reaching the front, he saw Eli was already with a customer. He also saw several customers were waiting. Lucas smiled, thinking about how so many people were already finding out about the shop, even though Eli had only been open for two days—as far as *he* could tell, anyway.

Eli stopped his conversation with the elderly gentleman and gestured toward Lucas. "This is my associate, Lucas Van der Meer."

The Dutchman nodded as Eli added, "Lucas, this is Mr. Diamini. He needs his shoes repaired."

Lucas picked up the shoes and began inspecting them, and the gentleman interjected, "I told Eli the shoes are so old, I am afraid they are irreparable. But they have carried me through many difficult times in my life, and I was hoping that maybe . . ."

Eli held up his hand and looked into the man's eyes with compassion. "Mr. Diamini, sometimes our oldest things have the greatest value. My belief is that everything we have is sacred until we decide it is time for them to move on. I think we can do good things with these fine shoes."

He winked at Lucas and then grinned. "What do you think, trusty associate?"

Lucas paused, not knowing exactly what to say, but then he replied, "Mr. Diamini, we have the finest cobbler in the city here—Eli Tambo—who is known as the Cobbler of Cape Town. What he will do with these shoes will astound you. When they are returned, not only will they feel like new, *but you'll also* feel like new when you put them on."

The older man was overjoyed. "I would . . . love that," he said quietly.

Lucas tagged the shoes and then carefully placed them behind the counter as Eli said to the customer, "We shall see you in two days, and your new shoes will be waiting for you." He grinned as the gentleman pivoted and walked happily out of the shop.

As the door shut, Lucas wore an astonished expression. "Eli, I am not sure what just happened there, but I think that was a . . . "

Eli finished his sentence. "A spiritual experience."

Lucas nodded in agreement. "Yes, it was *spiritual*, that's exactly what it was."

Eli nodded also and then added, "Which is exactly what was necessary. He needs his shoes repaired, but more importantly, he needs his *spirit* repaired. It was a start."

Lucas's enthusiasm could not be contained. "Most customers would be happy to even get a neutral response as they handed their shoes over to a cobbler. Your words gave that man . . . hope. It's as if you knew he was in pain, and you genuinely cared."

Eli shrugged. "Each person we meet is in pain, Lucas—whether it's discernable or not."

The cobbler smiled gently, then turned to see the other two customers that Lucas had noticed previously. They were standing outside the shop, and when Mr. Diamini left, they walked in. The two ladies strolled to the counter and smiled.

"May we help you?" Lucas happily offered.

The first woman responded, "I am Nomusa Mabunda, and this is my sister Thandeka. We met a woman from Durban yesterday who had just visited your shop, and she said it was a wonderful experience. We wanted to see what the fuss was about, and I must say, the older gentleman who just left could not stop talking about you two."

Eli smiled. "Well, we aim to please."

Thandeka quickly chimed in, "With the way life has become in this country for us—the horror of it all—to have a small beacon of happiness is exactly what we need. When did you open your shop?"

Lucas shot a quick glance toward Eli.

"Well, sometimes it seems like forever. But I'm really the new kid on the block to most folks." He grinned.

The ladies laughed, and then Nomusa replied, "Well, new kid, here are our shoes. Can they be salvaged?" With that, the women placed two pairs of white heels on the counter. The shoes had seen better days, no doubt about it.

Eli looked at Lucas, who carefully picked up and examined the footwear. "Indeed, these shoes have seen great life events, but I believe the Cobbler of Cape Town can help them see many more." He grinned broadly at Eli.

The cobbler chuckled. "I think you're right, Lucas. I bet we can make them better than ever." He turned to the ladies and added, "Plus, I think you two will look absolutely stunning in them."

The ladies squealed with delight, and then Thandeka spoke. "Mr. Eli, I must say, I didn't have any hope for these shoes being able to be brought back to life. But not only that, I feel like this is bringing *us* back to life. My sister and I have been through traumatic times recently—the government resettled us from our lifelong homes two weeks ago. Most of our belongings were lost or destroyed in the displacement, but these two pairs of shoes were incredibly special to both of us as we wore them at our weddings years ago. Both of our husbands are deceased, and these high heels are the only reminders we have left."

The other woman cut in, tears rolling down her cheeks. "To be able now to see these things of such rare sentimental value restored—it is just unbelievable. Thank you both."

The men smiled in gratitude, then Eli replied, "It's an honor that you would bring them here, and you will be even more pleased when you pick them up on Friday. God bless you both, and may God save Cape Town."

The two ladies nodded in agreement, then walked out of the shop. When the door closed, Lucas turned to Eli in awe. "Amazing. They left here happier than when they arrived—to simply drop off shoes."

Eli shook his head. "They did not just drop off shoes. They dropped off some of their cares—if only for a few moments. If we can help people be relieved of their burdens for even a short period of time, then we are making a difference."

Lucas smiled. "I never would have thought cobbling could have the potential to impact someone's life at this deep of a level."

Eli thoughtfully responded, "It has less to do with the work, and more to do with the spirit of the worker. Of course, the quality must be present, but if the job is done without heart, there can be no real success."

Just then, Eli paused and looked around, as if he was hearing something. "Lucas, you need to go back to your hotel and make sure everything is okay."

Lucas squinched his face up. "What are you talking about?"

The cobbler shook his head. "No time to waste. Go over there, pack your things, and check out. Get back here as soon as you can."

The Dutchman was about to find out *exactly* what Eli meant . . .

CHAPTER 11

Lucas hurried across the street, and when he got to the front desk, the clerk immediately stood up, raised his hands, and addressed the young man in a distressed tone. "I am sorry, sir. They came so quickly and . . . what could I do? I didn't know how to reach you . . ."

Lucas didn't bother to ask questions. He turned and ran up the stairs and down the hallway to his room where he found the door flung open. Pausing at the doorway, the young man surveyed the scene, and what he saw sent a chill down his spine. His belongings were scattered across the floor, and the entire room was in disarray—as if someone had been frantically searching for something.

But for what? he thought to himself. *Who could have done this—and why would they do it?*

Then he saw it on the floor near the window. The framed picture he had of his mother and father was crushed, and the picture was nearly torn in half. Lucas picked up the broken mass tenderly as pieces of the frame crumbled in his hands. He gazed longingly at the photograph, and tears began to well up.

At that moment, the hotel clerk appeared in the room and saw the terrible scene.

"Who did this?" Lucas screamed.

The clerk shook his head. "The police. They didn't tell me what they were searching for, only that they needed to see what was in your room. I had no choice but to let them in."

"I just . . . don't understand," Lucas lamented.

"It is the way of life here, Mr. Van der Meer. We have no privacy, and we have few rights. We are second-class citizens who belong to the state of South Africa."

The clerk began to clean up the mess, but Lucas motioned him away. "I will handle this. I am afraid I must leave the hotel—but thank you for your hospitality."

The clerk bowed respectfully to Lucas, then turned and slowly walked back down the stairs to his desk.

Lucas hastily pulled his belongings together, put them in his suitcase, and headed downstairs. When he reached the lobby, he walked past the front desk and called to the clerk, "Please tell Joseph the server I said goodbye. I pray that we will all find better days ahead."

The clerk nodded, and now with a tone of regret, he replied, "It is my prayer also, Mr. Van der Meer. Thank you . . ."

Lucas held on tightly to his suitcase as he walked across the street to the cobbler's shop. Opening the front door, he found Eli at the desk, quietly tagging shoes. The old man stopped and looked tenderly at Lucas. "I am sorry."

"How did you know, Eli?"

Eli shrugged. "There are times I just . . . know. I don't question how that is, but I do know intuition has saved me more than once. I am only sad I could not keep you from having experienced what just happened." He continued, "Lucas, I would like you to come stay with me. You will have your own room, and I believe you'll find it is quite comfortable in my home. I feel like we will be able to share experiences, and I will be able to help you learn about what is happening in South Africa."

Lucas hesitated and then meekly replied, "Eli, I'm so humbled by your gesture, but I don't want to take advantage of you and your generosity."

The older man shook his head, waved his hand dismissively, and smiled. "Nonsense. After all, we cobblers need to stick together. Plus," he said as he reached behind the desk and pulled out a stack of papers, "it's about to get busy around here, so the closer to the shop you are, the better."

Lucas's eyes became like saucers. "Are those work orders?"

Eli nodded and flashed a toothy grin. "In the hour you were gone, we had eight new orders."

"I don't believe it. How are these people finding out about you?" he gasped.

"About *us*," Eli countered. "Apparently people are pleased with the work and with the service, so . . . I guess they are telling their friends."

"One person at a time, just like you told me earlier. Changing the world one person at a time." Lucas beamed.

Just then, a customer came in to pick up her shoes. It was the older woman Lucas had met shortly after he met Eli. She now walked in cheerfully—unlike on her previous visit.

She began, "I can't explain it. I just felt so inspired when I left your shop. After grieving my mother's death, I needed to feel some care and compassion. Who would have guessed I would find *that* at a cobbler's shop? I couldn't wait to come back."

Eli smiled and shrugged. "Well, we do like to keep our customers satisfied." He walked a few steps over to a shelf near the desk, reached up to the third row, and pulled down two pairs of shoes.

"I believe these are yours," he said as he handed them to the woman.

She carefully inspected the shoes, and her heart seemed to leap. "I can't believe it. They look . . . brand new. I don't know how to repay you."

Eli and Lucas exchanged smiles. "Lucas, would you mind ringing this up? I think it's only six pence."

"Gladly," Lucas replied as he reached for the register keys.

The woman took her receipt, thanked Eli again, and headed for the door. However, she stopped and turned back, just before she reached the doorway. "I hope you don't mind; I've told my friends about you, and I think the shop may get even busier very soon." Her eyes sparkled.

Eli looked at Lucas and then turned back to the woman with an appreciative countenance. "No problem, ma'am. I've got this young man's energy to go with my experience. We're ready . . . and thank you."

The three of them laughed together, and the patron then headed out the door into the warm Cape Town afternoon.

Lucas put his hand on the cobbler's shoulder. "Eli, I've been thinking. I would be honored to move into the room you have. I can already tell there is so much I can learn from you, and having a place to stay will take a huge load off my mind."

Eli nodded. "I think it will be a perfect fit. Come on, let's knock off a little early, and we'll head over there right now so you can see where it's located."

With that, Eli stepped over and changed the sign to CLOSED, grabbed his bicycle, and the two men walked out of the shop.

As they left, Eli began walking with the bike next to him as Lucas strolled alongside. Looking toward the young apprentice, the cobbler offered, "It won't take us long to get there, and we can stop along the way to grab a bite to eat for when we get home."

"Sounds great, I'm starved," Lucas said as he smiled and rubbed his stomach.

"Bottomless pit, huh? I think your mum was right." Eli beamed at Lucas, who was also smiling broadly.

For the first time since he had been in South Africa, Lucas Van der Meer felt a little bit at home, and *that* was a feeling he desperately needed.

CHAPTER 12

After a quick stop at the butcher shop, Eli and Lucas made it to the house, which was a small, attractive, white structure made of wood, with a neatly manicured yard. They walked in, and Eli placed the bag of meat on the kitchen counter. Lucas followed close behind him, suitcase in his hand.

"Let me show you to your room, my friend," Eli offered.

Lucas nodded and smiled appreciatively before following Eli. The interior of the home was about twelve hundred square feet, all on one level. As they strolled through it, Lucas observed how all the rooms were simply and tastefully decorated. He also noted there was a cheerful energy that seemed to permeate the entire dwelling.

Once they reached the guest room, Eli walked in first, and with a sweeping gesture, announced, "May I present the Lucas Van der Meer Suite!" He grinned.

Lucas gazed around the room and noticed how the soft blue color of the walls blended with the bedspread and the white-and-blue pillows. There was also perfect symmetry of the various pictures on the wall, and the knick-knacks were precisely placed throughout.

Setting down the suitcase, Lucas shook his head in disbelief. "It feels so comfortable to me already. I'm grateful, Eli."

The cobbler nodded and patted the young man kindly on the back. "I'm glad you like it. Why don't you wash up and take a few minutes to relax, then I'll meet you in the kitchen for dinner in, let's say, thirty minutes?"

"Sounds great," the young man affirmed.

Eli walked out, and Lucas began unpacking, lost in thought about the last two days. From the unexpected events on his cab ride, to the police tearing apart his room at the hotel, to everything he had now learned about oppressive South African laws—he was exhausted just thinking about it all.

But . . . then he reflected on the times at the shop with Eli. It was as if this man had the ability to make everything better for everyone he met. No matter the scenario, Eli maintained a relaxed, contagiously optimistic attitude. He seemed sure everything that was happening was simply part of a bigger plan, and it was almost as if he *knew* what that plan was.

In fact, as crazy as it sounded, it was like Eli Tambo had known Lucas was going to be showing up in Cape Town all along . . .

Lucas put that thought aside as he placed his last few items in one of the drawers and then put his suitcase in the closet. Glancing at the clock, he realized it was about time to head into the kitchen as Eli had asked. He ambled down the hallway, again taking in his new surroundings. Everything was so clean and bright—a refreshing change from his hotel room.

When he reached the kitchen, he found Eli cooking. Sensing the approach of Lucas, the older man turned around and smiled. "Well, are you all settled?"

"Yes indeed. It really is already feeling like home—thank you."

Eli nodded and then turned back to his cooking. "I fixed a little bit of chicken, along with some carrots and peppers for dinner. Hope that's okay."

Lucas rubbed his hands together in approval. "Mmmm, sounds perfect!"

After a few moments, Eli brought the meal over to the small wooden table where he had already set the places for dinner. Motioning for Lucas to sit down, the man then piled a generous serving of all the offerings onto the young man's plate. He then scooped out a more modest amount onto his own plate and placed the pan with the leftovers on the stove.

Eli sat down, and after he voiced a short blessing, the two men began enjoying their meals. At one point, Lucas stopped eating, put down his fork, and with a philosophical tone, asked Eli, "How do you think everything will unfold with this community—and the country?"

Eli paused and then thoughtfully replied, "Lucas, I am simply a cobbler. I don't know *exactly* what the future holds here. What I *do* know is that the power of good always wins over evil—always. Now, *how* that will happen here, I can't say. But I believe our job is to use our gifts to empower, encourage, and connect people—to make a positive impact in their lives. The ripple effect of that can eventually be monumental as far as shifting the culture and creating a climate of change."

Then Eli propped his elbows on the table, laced his fingers, and added evenly, "But, my friend, this work will not be easy, I can assure you."

Lucas palmed the back of his neck as he noted the intensity of Eli's words. He then looked pensively at his mentor and responded in a measured way. "I understand. I have wondered many times since I left Amsterdam why I'm here. The longer I am here, and the more time I spend with you, the closer I feel I am to the answer to that nagging question."

The cobbler smiled slightly, nodded, and took another bite of chicken.

Lucas pivoted in the direction of his questions. "Eli, what do you think is the craving all these people have that come into the shop? Is it happiness? You have helped me understand that the answer is not just related to shoes. Whatever it is, they are leaving feeling better about their lives."

Eli gave a half shrug. "On the surface, they want to be happy, of course. But underneath that, I think they are searching for something a bit different."

Lucas leaned forward in interest as Eli continued. "People want to feel valued, Lucas, and there is so much in this country—and maybe even in the world—that leads to people feeling anything but valued."

The Dutchman nodded his understanding.

"There are times in people's lives when they feel misunderstood, unappreciated, unwanted, and undeserving. That is what is happening daily here in Cape Town to our fellow citizens, and it's precisely the *opposite* of what people feel when they come into the shop. When they leave, I hope each person feels like they were the most important person in the world to us at that moment. The result of that type of experience is almost indescribable as far as the power it generates."

Lucas chimed in, "Plus, it's contagious."

The cobbler pointed at him excitedly and smiled. "Exactly! In fact, when we go back tomorrow, I can almost assure you that we will see the manifestation of that contagiousness."

Lucas raised an eyebrow. "How so?"

Eli leaned back in his chair and shook his head as the corners of his mouth turned up. "Wait and see. As I said before, I can't tell you the future—even what the future holds for the next day. But I do know people, and when we are doing the right, unselfish things with pure motives, good results will happen—and maybe happen quickly."

The two men continued to enjoy the dinner and their engaging conversation. The more the discussion continued, the more Lucas realized he had been blessed not only with a close, much-needed friend but also a teacher with extraordinary, life-enhancing gifts.

As the clock struck eight, the pair realized they had been sitting and talking for over three hours—and the time seemed to have flown by. They each pushed away from the table and began the process of cleaning up, then washing and putting away the dishes.

Once their work was done, Lucas glanced at the clock and yawned. "I think I'll turn in a little early tonight, Eli. It's been a long day—a great day, but a long one."

The cobbler flashed one of his relaxed, comforting smiles. "That's probably a good idea. As I said, I have a feeling tomorrow is going to be a big day for us."

Lucas nodded and smiled in agreement, but as he turned to walk away, he heard Eli quietly add, "A very, very big day . . ."

CHAPTER 13

Lucas was pleasantly surprised that he slept blissfully through the night. He could only assume the fact that Eli had been so kind in bringing him into his home, plus giving him a job, had provided some much-needed peace after these grueling two weeks of insecurity.

It was around 7:30 when he walked into the kitchen to find Eli standing by the coffee pot, pouring them both a piping hot cup of goodness. The older man turned and handed the drink to Lucas.

"Let's take the coffee with us. We'll walk to the shop and have a muffin along the way as we talk."

Lucas nodded, then the pair took their food and drink and walked out the door to begin the short trip to the store.

After a few minutes, Eli asked with a mischievous smile, "You mentioned that you came by steamship most of the way. Did you meet anyone onboard?"

Lucas shook his head and smiled back at the man. "It's like you know *everything*—and the answer is yes, I did meet a young woman . . ."

Eli's eyes twinkled. "Ah, I see."

"Yes, but she wasn't just *any* woman. She seemed, well, she seemed to know me—at my very core."

"The best kind of woman, I would say," Eli offered back with a broad smile.

Lucas grinned, but then the happiness seemed to fade. "Anyway . . . I have a feeling I'll never see her again."

Eli appeared not to understand. "Why is that?"

"It seems her mother felt I was not 'appropriate' for her daughter, because of my skin color."

Eli nodded and continued to listen.

"I would give anything to just see her. She crosses my mind every day . . . do you think I might ever find her? She's from Cape Town."

Eli rubbed his chin, thinking deeply as the pair continued to walk. "Well, like I have said, I don't know what tomorrow holds, but I do know if you are meant to be together . . . you will be."

Lucas's eyes widened as he excitedly turned again toward Eli.

"I can't think of anything better! It would be the ultimate gift just to look in her beautiful blue eyes again. It's strange how someone can have a powerful impact on you in such a short period of time . . ."

Right then, the men happened upon two women sweeping the sidewalk in front of a residence. Seeing Eli and Lucas, they stopped their task, and each of them raised a hand in greeting. One of the women turned to her friend and said, "That's him! That's the cobbler!"

"Did you hear that?" Lucas asked incredulously. "She is probably the third person I have seen on our short trip who has recognized you. Do you know these folks?"

Eli waved to the excited ladies. Then turning back to Lucas, he whispered with a grin, "Not yet. But hopefully we'll know every person in this community soon."

Lucas nodded and offered an approving smile. Then he put his hand over his eyes to shield them from the morning sun and peered into the distance. "Eli, the shop is just ahead, and . . . do you see what I see? We don't open for twenty more minutes, but there is a line in front of about twenty people!"

Eli craned his neck to see, then his eyes sparkled as he cheerfully replied, "Seems like you are going to be a busy boy today!" He slapped Lucas affectionately on the back, and the two quickened their pace.

Once they approached the shop, the buzz of the crowd became louder. "Hello, Eli! Good morning, Lucas!" People were calling to the two as if they were all longtime friends.

Eli walked up the steps to the shop, then turned and smiled as he addressed the gathering. "Ah, what a way to start my day, with the finest citizens in Cape Town choosing to be at my front door! Please give us just a few moments to get the shop ready for opening. We'll have you on your way in no time!"

With that, Eli unlocked the door, then quickly locked it again behind them as the two entered.

"It's just like you said it would be—busier than yesterday!" Lucas breathed excitedly.

Eli shook his head and flashed a teasing grin. "Well, even though I am not a fortune teller . . . I had a hunch."

The two men quickly prepared the shop for opening, then Lucas reached up, turned the sign to OPEN, and unlocked the door.

The young associate walked out and held up his hands to the growing group of customers. "One guest at a time, please. It's a small shop, and we want to give each person our full attention." He smiled at Eli, who was nodding his approval.

Lucas held the door open for the first guest, a middle-aged man wearing a gray suit and a coordinated top hat. Entering the shop, he tipped his hat to Lucas, who then closed the door behind the visitor.

The gentleman approached the counter and said politely to Eli, "I would like to pick up some shoes for my father. He came in recently, but you may not remember him. As he began describing his father to Eli, the cobbler interrupted, "Yes, of course, Mr. Diamini! He was one of my first customers!"

The man nodded and smiled. "Yes, that's what he told me."

The gentleman waited while Eli went to the rear of the shop to retrieve the shoes. In just a moment, he returned to the front, repaired footwear in hand. "Here you are, friend. That will be ten pence. I hope your father will enjoy them, and please share that it was my pleasure to meet him. You may pay Lucas at the other end of the counter."

The man turned to do so, then he turned back to the cobbler. "Mr. Tambo . . ." He hesitated, and a thoughtful look came across his face as Eli now wrinkled his brow in curiosity about the forthcoming words.

"I just want to say . . . thank you."

Eli cocked his head. "For the shoes? Well, of course, it's my pleasure."

The gentleman shook his head, and Lucas now turned to listen.

"Mr. Tambo, the shoes are indeed beautiful—your craftsmanship is impeccable. However, what you have done for my father is even more extraordinary. You see, he is very ill, and the doctor has given him only a short period of time to live. However, what you have given him is . . . dignity."

Eli focused intently as the man continued.

"The shoes are very important to him—they were given to him as a special gift many years ago in his working days. My mother used to tell him how handsome he looked in them, and it always made him so happy to hear that. He treasures those shoes, and hearing they would be back in beautiful condition was especially meaningful in these final days."

The man hesitated, then said, "He left your shop encouraged and feeling loved—as odd as that may sound."

Eli smiled appreciatively and put his hand on the man's shoulder. "Your father is a special person, and I could quickly see that. It was an honor to have him here, and I hope you will let him know it would be an honor to have him come back any time and see us."

Lucas nodded in admiration as he listened to the brief interaction. *Yes*, he thought, *there is something incredibly special about this place . . . and this man, Eli Tambo.*

The gentleman then paid the young associate, shook his hand, and smiled as he walked out the door.

Lucas followed right behind him and stepped out to invite the next guest in. A young woman entered, and when she did, Lucas lingered outside for a moment, noticing more and more people had joined the queue. But then, scanning the area, he noticed something else . . . the region in general was busier and seemed to have much more energy than it previously had. Across the street, more people were walking into the hotel with suitcases in hand, and even more people pouring into the hotel simply to go to the restaurant. *Strange*, he thought to himself. He turned and walked back into the store, closing the door behind himself.

Eli was at the counter, fully engaged with the young customer. The cobbler nodded, smiled, asked her a few questions, listened carefully to her responses, then took her shoes in exchange for the claim ticket. As Lucas walked toward them, Eli and the woman finished their conversation, then she turned and smiled at the approaching young man as she strolled out the door.

Lucas shook his head and laughed. "Well, clearly another satisfied customer—or should I say, clearly another *happy person*."

Eli chuckled. "Well, these people make it especially easy to work with them. They all seem so . . . kind. They are like friends, not just customers."

Lucas shrugged. "I would say it's more a case of the old saying, 'To make a friend, you must be friendly'—and that is precisely what you are, Eli."

The African flashed a broad grin. "Well, you haven't seen me on my bad days." The two men laughed, and the next customer entered the shop and was treated in the same, special way.

Indeed, that was how the whole day went; a customer would come in, have a uniquely wonderful experience, and leave feeling like a better person. Or maybe . . . they *were* better people.

At one point in the afternoon, there was a small break with no customers in the store, which gave the two men a chance to catch their breath. At that moment, the server from the hotel restaurant across the street showed up carrying two large bags of food. Lucas recognized him immediately. "Joseph, it's so great to see you!" The two young men shook hands, then Lucas introduced him to Eli, whom the server graciously acknowledged before setting the food on the counter.

Gesturing toward the two sacks, Joseph said, "I thought you guys might like a little bite to eat, so I brought you some of today's special from the kitchen—it's good, I promise. But unfortunately, we ran out of shark." He grinned as Lucas jokingly rolled his eyes.

The waiter's tone then became more serious as he said, "Plus, I wanted to thank you."

Lucas and Eli exchanged quizzical glances as Joseph continued, "I mean, thank you for what is happening. The hotel is getting incredibly busy—as is most of the district—and it's all thanks to what you two are doing here. I am not sure what your recipe is, but look outside the door." He turned and gestured toward the street.

Eli and Lucas followed his gesture and saw what the young man was referring to. Citizens were greeting each other in the street, shaking hands, laughing, listening to each other. There was more traffic on the road, and people were playing with their children as they walked down the sidewalk.

"You would never see jubilance like that before—even just last week. Parents would not smile with their children. They just wanted to get home as quickly as possible and hide from the world. Now, it's as if they want to be *part* of the world—a new world of hope, it seems. In fact, to the left of your shop, there is a market going in the space. The buildout just started today."

The two men stuck their heads out the door and immediately saw the construction.

"Plus," he continued, "on the other side, there is a new dry-cleaning shop arriving soon. It's like that all up and down the street and continuing through much of District Six."

Smiles spread across the faces of Eli and Lucas. The young server said, "Speaking of more business, I've got to get back to the restaurant. It's really hopping in there today—but I just wanted to quickly drop by and say thanks." With that, Joseph dashed out the door and disappeared across the street into the hotel.

Eli and Lucas opened the bags of food on the counter to find two roast beef sandwiches and fried potatoes, which the men devoured.

Eli then folded his arms, leaned back against the wall, and asked Lucas with curiosity in his voice, "What do you think about his comments on the area's transformation?"

Lucas hesitated, then crumpled up the bag and threw it in the trash can behind the desk. "Eli, I'm just a cobbler's apprentice, but . . . I would say there are some *miraculous* things happening around here." He laughed.

Eli grinned. "Well, I'm certainly a believer in miracles."

Lucas nodded and chuckled. "I am starting to believe in them also, my friend." He shook his head playfully as he turned and walked to the back of the store.

Just then, a customer entered the shop. She was a shapely young woman, no older than twenty. Fully covered by a long-sleeved, full-length white dress and gloves, she also wore a light pink, flat-brimmed hat, tilted to one side. Her eyes were concealed behind large, circular, gold-rimmed sunglasses, and the combination of the dress and accessories meant none of her skin was revealed to the hot Cape Town sun.

The woman slowly approached the counter and handed Eli a magnificent pair of red high-heeled shoes.

She spoke softly. "I would like these repaired, please."

Eli hesitated and wrinkled his brow, as if he recognized the woman. Sensing this, she quickly averted her gaze.

Noting the young lady's nervousness, Eli's tone was especially gentle as he continued, "I have to say the shoes look perfect, ma'am. Are you sure they're in need of repair?"

She managed a half smile. "Sometimes things which seem beautiful on the outside have a great need to be repaired on the inside."

Eli smiled knowingly and nodded. "I have a feeling my associate cobbler can help in this case."

Hearing that last sentence as he walked to the front, Lucas looked quizzically toward the woman as Eli handed her a ticket. "Please give this to the young man at the other end of the counter."

Nodding, she took the piece of paper and her gaze turned down as she inched over toward Lucas, who was now positioned back at his typical post near the register. As she gave him the ticket, she removed her sunglasses, and Lucas's eyes became wide. "Victoria!" He rushed to get around the counter and threw his arms around the clearly ecstatic girl as she then held onto him tightly.

"Lucas, I *knew* it was you. I have been hearing about the cobbler and his apprentice—even from people in Table Mountain where I live. When people describe the handsome, kind young man . . . I had to come see for myself. I'm so happy I found you." Tears trickled down her pale white cheeks.

The two continued to embrace, and finally Lucas pulled away. Turning toward his mentor, he excitedly blurted out, "Eli, this is Victoria—the woman I have told you so much about!"

Although Eli smiled, he had an oddly subdued response—almost as if it wasn't the first time he had met her. "It's a pleasure, ma'am. Lucas has indeed said many wonderful things about you. Now, if you will excuse me, I'll give you two some time together—I'm sure you won't be able to stay long, as I know you understand it's not safe." With that, Eli nodded goodbye, turned, and then walked to the rear of the shop and out of sight.

Concern in his eyes, Lucas added, "Victoria, he's right—it's not safe for you here."

She shook her head dismissively. "Lucas, I've missed you so much. I've thought about our time together every day since I last saw you."

Lucas grinned. "It's been the same for me." Then his smile faded as he added, "I . . . I was afraid we would never see each other again."

Victoria squeezed the young man's hands and lovingly gazed into his eyes. "I knew we would find each other at some point, Lucas. I just knew it."

Right then, Lucas looked at Victoria's hands as they held his.

"Victoria . . . your engagement ring . . . it's gone. Are you—?"

She interrupted and shook her head. "I broke the engagement off. In my heart, it never felt right to go through with it . . . then when I met you, I *knew* he was not right for me."

Lucas swallowed.

He grabbed the young woman and held her tightly again, as if to never let her go. Yet then, he abruptly pulled away and stared blankly into the distance.

Surprised, Victoria asked, "What is it, Lucas?"

"Victoria, I'm so happy to see you again. But Eli is right—it's dangerous, and I couldn't live with myself if anything happened to you. I will escort you to the borderline of the district, and then you will need to get a cab back to your home."

She hesitated, and then her gaze fell to the floor as she shook her head. "No, I will make my way. I am more familiar with the route back than you. But Lucas . . . I came here also because there's something I must tell you."

Lucas furrowed his brow in confusion. "What is it?"

"What you and Eli are doing here is truly incredible. I am astounded to see the love and strength and comradery that is visibly taking hold of this community, but trust me . . . you must be careful. There are people who aren't excited about the success and happiness that are starting to occur in this area of Cape Town."

Lucas furrowed his brow again, still unsure of where the conversation was going. "What do you mean?"

"I can't explain now, but just know . . . you and Eli must be extremely cautious in this noble work you're engaged in. Now, as you said, I must go—but we will meet again. I promise."

With that, the young woman put on her sunglasses and walked quickly outside to a waiting car. As she approached the vehicle, the driver opened the rear passenger door, stepped back, and saluted her.

Lucas, having walked out of the shop to watch her go, now cocked his head, puzzled by what he was seeing. As Victoria quickly stepped into the shiny automobile, she took one last glance back toward Lucas and then motioned for the driver to close the door.

As the car pulled away, Lucas felt his head spinning, reflecting on everything that had just happened so quickly.

Then Victoria's words echoed in his mind: "*There are some people who aren't excited about the success and happiness that are starting to occur in this area of Cape Town.*"

Lucas Van der Meer exhaled loudly and looked heavenward as he suddenly wondered just how prepared for this journey he really was . . .

CHAPTER 14

Walking back into the shop, Lucas saw Eli sitting at the front counter, going through the day's receipts.

The cobbler looked up and asked with a twinkle in his eyes, "How did it go?"

Lucas shook his head. "I can't believe she was here." Then he paused, confused. "But, Eli . . . you almost seemed like you weren't surprised to see her."

Eli shrugged and arched an eyebrow. "Oh, I was surprised, alright. Lucas . . . do you know who that was?"

The young man gave his mentor a bewildered glance and then said in frustration, "What do you mean? Eli, this was the girl from the boat that I've been telling you about."

Eli reached deliberately behind the counter and retrieved an old Cape Town newspaper, then he turned to the second page and pointed halfway down the copy to a photograph.

Lucas's eyes were instantly glued to the picture. It was . . . Victoria. She was standing beside a familiar man who appeared to be in his fifties, and there was also a woman with them whom Lucas immediately recognized as Victoria's mother.

Eli shrugged. "Yes, it *was* the girl from the boat. Also known as Victoria Lubbers, the daughter of Arend Lubbers—the mayor of Cape Town. You haven't been here long enough to know who he is, but that's him standing beside Victoria and her mother."

The light brown color seemed to drain from Lucas's face. "What? Yes, I knew her last name was Lubbers, but I had no idea. . ." His voice trailed off.

Eli nodded and handed him the paper. "As you've been telling me all along about her, I had a strange feeling that might be the case. She's well known in Cape Town, and not just because she's Arend Lubbers's daughter."

Lucas cocked his head, listening, as Eli continued.

"Victoria is well known and even loved in this community for her views on inclusion. Her parents—especially her father—are staunch segregationists, and they are not happy in the least with her perspective. It's why she was in Europe also."

"What do you mean?"

"The word on the street is they wanted her away from Cape Town once she became engaged. Her fiancé is from a 'proper' South African family, and his views are like those of Mayor and Mrs. Lubbers. Apparently, Victoria was having serious doubts about the marriage, and the parents thought they could take her to Europe for a little while to 'get her head on straight.' So, her mother took Victoria ostensibly to visit family, but really to try and get her to start thinking more like them—and like her new fiancé."

Lucas hung his head and shook it in despair. "No wonder Victoria's mum hated me. I pretty much spoiled their plan." Then he looked back up at Eli and added, "But, I'll have to say, from what Victoria just shared with me, her mum is going to have to get used to—"

Eli held up his hand and cut in. "Well, actually . . ."

"Actually *what*?" Lucas shot back.

"I heard a rumor that Victoria's mother passed away."

The young man gaped at Eli, genuinely shocked. "A rumor?"

The older cobbler shook his head and raised his shoulders. "The politicians keep any news out of our papers that might make them appear less than immortal. We often don't find out about significant life-or-death events for months—or longer. So yes, it's just a rumor."

Still clearly perplexed, Lucas started to follow up on his question, but before he could speak, another customer entered the shop. Eli subtly pointed at Lucas and added quietly, "We'll talk more about this later."

The young man nodded, and then both turned their attention to the heavyset, dark-skinned woman walking in.

"My goodness," she said, "I can't believe how many people are on the street here now—and so many new stores! Is it true that this place is responsible for the growth and excitement? I mean, it is just a cobbler shop . . . isn't it?"

Eli shrugged and smiled. "That it is, ma'am. However, I think you'll find that this shop is one you'll remember. At least, that's our goal." He winked.

"Very good. Well, I do have some sandals that need help." She reached into a bag and pulled out a pair of worn, discolored wooden sandals that did indeed seem as if they were in distress.

Lucas walked over and squinted at the shoes which Eli was now carefully assessing. The young associate wondered aloud, "Where did these shoes come from?"

She paused as if surprised by his question. "Zambia. What made you ask?"

Lucas looked knowingly at Eli, then gestured toward the sandals. "May I see them?"

Eli obliged and handed the sandals to the young man.

After examining the footwear thoroughly, Lucas nodded. "Zambia, yes, that's what I thought."

The woman smiled. "So, you recognize these are not typical shoes?"

The apprentice nodded. "Absolutely. The craftsmanship from this Zambian cobbler is unlike any other—Eli has told me a great deal about the man's work, but I have never actually seen anything he has done."

The woman smiled and nodded in agreement. "I have never known a cobbler I would trust to repair them. I was told that you two might be able to help since I want my daughter to have these one day, and then hopefully she can pass them on to *her* daughter in the future. The cobbler was a friend of my grandfather, and the shoes were a gift when I was born. The Zambian cobbler has long since died, but his work, as you said, was impeccable."

Eli took the sandals and turned them over, then pointed to some words that were etched into the underside. "He embedded a unique African phrase in each masterpiece he cobbled."

Lucas nodded and smiled. "Yes indeed, look at that . . ."

Staring at the etching, Eli shrugged. "I am not too familiar with this language, but . . ."

The woman smiled, then held up her hand to gently interrupt him. She read the markings and translated the words. "'May God give love, peace, and happiness to the woman who wears these sandals—and may she share those gifts wherever she travels in them.'"

Eli shook his head in awe. "Beautiful words, and as you can see, the materials he chose are exquisite. He only used rare Central African white aspen trees to create his shoes. It's an honor that you would bring them here for us to work on."

She grinned, visibly pleased that Eli and Lucas had heard of the Zambian cobbler. "I was hoping I would someday be led to a place that could give these shoes the care they need and deserve. It appears that is exactly what I have found."

Eli glanced at Lucas and then turned back to the woman. "The sandals will be stunning when they are finished, although there is a type of *wabi-sabi* in them that makes them gorgeous as-is."

The visitor arched an eyebrow as if she did not understand.

"It is Japanese for 'perfection in imperfection.' Everything has something about it that is not perfect in the eyes of the world. However, one who can discern things spiritually knows that imperfection is what gives the item its soul."

The woman nodded. "Well, whether the shoes appear perfect or not, I would say they do have a spiritual element to them. So, I will be excited to see what condition they are in when you return them to me."

She looked at Eli, then at Lucas. "May I come back in a week?"

Eli smiled. "Your spiritual shoes will be waiting."

When the customer walked out, Lucas turned to his mentor and said quietly, "Okay, so you're a Zen master, too. That was . . . amazing."

Eli shook his head and laughed. "I am simply—"

Lucas held up his hand to stop him and said, "I know, I know, you're simply a cobbler." He grinned.

Eli shrugged his shoulders and beamed, then the next customer entered the shop and received a similarly wonderful experience, as did each person who arrived after that. Visitors would feel renewed, inspired, and empowered, and they would leave and tell their friends about the encounter. Each day there was more growth in their business—and in the area. The entire community was not only beginning to flourish, but it was also clearly being *transformed*.

One afternoon in the shop as they were repairing shoes, Eli stopped and turned to Lucas. "I have an idea."

The Dutchman smiled. "What's that?"

"I think we should take a few days and go out to the savannah. You'll find the scenery is breathtaking, and we can have some long-overdue conversations."

Lucas tilted his head, appearing surprised. "But . . . the shop. We'll lose so much money!"

Eli hesitated, then said kindly to the young man, "I think we'll gain much more than we'll lose."

With that, Eli put a note on the door to customers, turned the sign to CLOSED, and motioned to Lucas. "Come on, let's go home and pack. We're going to have some full days."

Lucas smiled broadly, and the two men then stepped out the door and began their short trek back to the house. Once they arrived, they began thoughtfully packing their clothes for the next three days. At dinner, the pair spent time excitedly talking about having a break from the business, but Eli also shared with Lucas some of the things he could expect.

"The savannahs are like nowhere else. The animals, the landscape, the plants and bushes, the sounds—it's not only mysterious, it's almost magical."

"*Magical.* I have a feeling you're going to be right about that, Eli. Ever since I was a little boy, I have wanted to see the fauna of southern Africa. Reading about it is one thing, but now getting to see it will be a life experience I know I'll always remember."

Eli nodded and then stood up from the table. "You won't be disappointed. Now, let's do a little tidying up around here before we turn in early—we'll leave shortly after dawn."

Lucas was feeling almost giddy, eager to see what excitement these upcoming days would hold . . .

CHAPTER 15

The next morning, the men woke up before sunrise and packed the last of their necessities, including the food they would take with them. Even though it was early, Lucas was already full of enthusiasm. "How will we get there, Eli? I know we're not going to use your bike!" He chuckled.

"Yes, that would be a little challenging." Eli grinned as he shook his head. "Actually, I have a friend who is a cab driver, and he is going to take us to an entrance for the savannah. We can hike from there to where we'll be making camp."

Just as he finished his sentence, they heard a honk outside. As Eli peered through the window, he saw his friend's taxi parked in the driveway.

"Yep, that's Shabi. Let's go," Eli urged. Picking up their backpacks, the pair walked out, closed the door, and jumped into the back of the cab. "Thanks for taking us, buddy." Eli reached up and patted the driver affectionately on the shoulder.

"Always a pleasure, Eli. Who is your friend?"

Pointing to Lucas, Eli said cheerfully, "Why, this is the next great cobbler in Cape Town, Lucas Van der Meer!"

"Ah, yes, I have heard of you also, Lucas. The young Dutchman!"

Lucas grinned. "That's me. Nice to meet you, Shabi. How do you and Eli know each other?"

Shabi smiled, pulled the cab out of the driveway, and replied, "Well, we go way back. Eli helped me with some challenges when I first entered the country from Madagascar. Times were horrible there, and when I got to South Africa, Eli made sure I met the right people, and he helped me get a job."

Eli smiled. "That was easy. A man like you would be welcome anywhere he was introduced."

Lucas cut in. "Well, it seems like Eli has a talent for bringing goodness into people's lives. I know he certainly has done that for me."

Shabi nodded. "Agreed, Lucas."

The men continued chatting and then a few minutes later, the driver took a right turn off the main street, and the cab headed down a dirt road out of town. "We'll have you there in no time. It's just getting light out, so sit back and take in the scenery."

Now that they were traveling away from the crowded city into the wilderness, there were fortunately fewer and fewer restrictions on where they could go. As Cape Town grew smaller in the distance, the scenery became increasingly rural, and there was great beauty in what they were seeing.

"Look!" Lucas shouted as he pointed off to the side. A large ostrich was making its way quickly down a path parallel to the road.

"Probably don't see a lot of those in Holland, do you?" Shabi cackled.

Lucas shook his head and grinned. "Um, no. If I saw one of those in Amsterdam, I would think I was losing my mind."

Eli chimed in, "They're pretty common out here." He then pointed in the distance and added, "Hey, take a look over to your right."

Lucas ventured a guess at what the animals were. "Coyotes?"

"No, they're hyenas. We'll want to steer clear of those," Eli said matter-of-factly. "Then again, they probably won't bother us if we don't bother them—like most things out here."

Lucas listened carefully as his wise friend continued. "Just watch your step, stay in your own lane, and everything will turn out okay."

At that point, the cabbie turned around and chipped in, "Especially with the snakes. They get a little . . . large out there." He shook his head and grinned.

"Yep, but you don't see many of those—or at least I haven't," Eli added casually as he continued to survey the passing landscape.

After a while, Shabi slowed the cab down and then pulled off on the side of the road. "Okay, Eli, this is the entrance that leads to the area you like. I'll let you guys take it from here."

The two travelers got out of the cab, and Eli walked around the front of the car to pay his friend.

"Nope, you know how much I owe *you*, Eli. This is on me. When would you like me to pick you two up from here?"

Eli blinked up at the sun. "We've probably got quite a few more hours of daylight today, so we can get to our site by this evening, and then we can spend all day tomorrow and tomorrow night. Maybe pick us up day after tomorrow about this time?"

The cabbie nodded and reached out the window to shake Eli's hand, and then the corners of his eyes crinkled as he addressed Lucas. "Enjoy your time. You've got one of the best guides in Africa."

Lucas nodded, then smiled at Eli. When the cab pulled away, the two men started down a well-worn path leading into the savannah.

As they forged ahead, Lucas was astounded at the rugged beauty of the African topography. He turned to Eli and asked, "So do you come here much?"

"Only when I want to push the world away for a while and have tranquility." He grinned.

"So, where are we?" Lucas persisted.

The eldest cobbler pointed just ahead. "We're right at the edge of a game reserve in northern South Africa. It's one of my favorite places. I can think so clearly here." Lucas nodded as Eli continued. "When I was small, my dad took me and my mother out here for weekends. At that time, there was seldom anyone that came to this area. Nowadays you'll occasionally see someone—mostly tribal people."

"Zulus?" Lucas offered.

"Exactly. Your South African history is better than I knew." He laughed.

"Well, I read a good bit about them in my Dutch history classes. The relationship Dutch settlers had with them was, um, not the best, I would say."

Eli threw back his head and laughed. "Yes, that's an understatement. When the Dutch settlers wanted to escape the British invaders, they pushed north into Zulu territory. The battles they fought were bloody on both sides."

"Okay, so I suppose I should keep quiet in case we see any Zulus, huh? I'm thinking they might not be too fond of my accent." He laughed nervously.

"That was a hundred years ago. I think you're okay now." Eli winked.

After about an hour, the journeymen reached a spot that seemed like it had been used by other campers. "This is where my dad used to take us—still looks the same," he added nostalgically.

With that, they took their packs off, laid out a few of their belongings, and surveyed the surroundings. "How about some water?" Eli suggested.

"Oh, man, that sounds great." Lucas reached for a canteen they had brought and downed a few big gulps.

"Wow, that's good!" Lucas licked his lips and smiled.

"Like gold, right? At least to a thirsty man, it is." Eli laughed.

They sat down on a couple of large rocks and rested. The silence was like nothing Lucas had ever experienced. "I can already tell why you like it here so much," Lucas said in a voice full of wonder.

Eli nodded and offered a sweeping gesture. "This is just the tip of it all. Come on, let me take you on a quick excursion."

Lucas shrugged and said with a grin, "Lead on, Cobbler of Cape Town."

"Yeah, yeah. Let's go, trusty associate . . ." Eli shook his head playfully and marched ahead, carefully walking through the thick bush and using a machete to clear the path. Eagles and osprey soared overhead as Lucas pointed in amazement. Eli smiled and nodded patiently.

A few moments later, a majestic herd of springboks bounced across the path about fifty yards in front of the men. Lucas was mesmerized by the graceful animals. "Look at that, Eli! There must be thirty of them!"

Eli also watched the beasts with awe. "The springbok is the national animal of South Africa. I never tire of watching them leap across the landscape." Then he seemed to reign his enthusiasm in as he added with a tone of caution, "There's lots to see, my friend, but pay attention to the path—that's where you really want to watch."

Lucas nodded his understanding.

A few moments later, the men came to an area that was buffered by a large stand of windblown trees. As they peeked around the trees, Eli turned to Lucas and smiled. About fifty yards ahead was a small lake. In and around the body of water were twelve magnificent elephants dominating the landscape. Eli held his finger to his lips and motioned for Lucas to move forward quietly. The two men crept ahead to a small hill just above the lake, which allowed for a clear perspective of the wild beasts.

"It's . . . incredible," Lucas whispered.

Eli nodded and replied quietly, "They've supposedly been coming here for hundreds of years. It's the place my dad would first take us when we arrived each visit."

Lucas shook his head in amazement, and then a few minutes later, Eli began backing up slowly, motioning for Lucas to do the same.

After about ten more steps, they were safely away from the herd, and Lucas began talking as he walked beside Eli. Still mindful of the volume of his voice, he breathed, "This has already been surreal, Eli. Thank you for bringing me here."

Eli beamed. "I'm glad you've liked it so far. There is so much to see, and there is such a sense of peace out here. It's one of the few places on Earth where you can find these exotic animals, and at the same time, also find a sense of solitude. I just love it."

"I can see why," Lucas concurred. "You know, you're lucky your father brought you out here. By the way, may I ask if your mother is still living?"

Eli shook his head gently. "She died about ten years after my father. I was blessed to have her for so long after he passed. The combination of their personalities made me the person I am grateful to be today."

"I know *I'm* sure grateful that you are who you are," Lucas returned with a smile.

The two continued to walk and take in the surroundings. At one point, Eli saw another springbok bouncing across the trail just in front of him. As it passed, the African stepped forward to more clearly see where the animal was headed.

But right then, Eli stopped.

Lucas immediately sensed a problem. "Hey, what happened, Eli? What's wrong?"

Then Lucas saw the source of Eli's sudden stillness. Only a few short steps in front of the cobbler, just off the path, was a snake Lucas immediately recognized. It was a dreaded puff adder, the most venomous snake on the continent and one of the deadliest in the world. The brown-and-beige serpent was now coiled, ready to strike.

For what seemed like minutes, Eli remained motionless, staring into the serpent's eyes as if he had no fear.

Lucas swallowed the lump in his throat as he stood transfixed, unable to help his friend.

Suddenly, the snake dropped out of its coiled position, deciding not to strike and instead slithering slowly off into the bush. At that point, the full size of the viper was clear to the two men. It was easily four feet long and likely ten inches in diameter. The brown-and-beige skin color had made the snake almost invisible beside the path, and if it had bitten Eli, the cobbler would surely have been dead within minutes.

Incredibly, Eli had a calm, unruffled look on his face as he turned to Lucas. "Ready to move on, my good man?"

Lucas gaped at him in disbelief. "'Ready to move on?' Eli, I am ready to throw up! Did you see what almost happened there?"

Eli now seemed to be enjoying the conversation. "Oh, trust me, I had quite a good view of what was happening there. I must say, that was a big one—and he was a little too close for comfort." He wiped his brow in jest and grinned.

Eli began walking on the trail again as if nothing had happened. Lucas picked up his pace to get beside him and then grabbed Eli by the shoulder. With wide eyes, he managed a faint smile, but then blurted out, "My friend, I was terrified! I wasn't even in the snake's line of sight, but it still scared me to death. How did you remain so calm?"

As if he didn't hear the question, Eli continued to walk. Then after a few seconds, he turned to the young man and said, "We have two choices—faith, or fear. Being consumed by fear is the real killer, Lucas. I have chosen faith in so many potentially frightening situations, it is simply a habit now. Was I afraid at first? Well, sure, and I was startled and even shocked. However, I have a mission, and now every frightening thing that gets put in my path quickly becomes another opportunity to become more mentally prepared for what I have been called to do. I've chosen to let go of all thoughts that don't make me stronger."

Lucas pursed his lips and then said in determination, "I want to be that way, Eli."

Eli's pensive gaze made it seem as if the statement deeply resonated with him. "You will be, Lucas. You will be very soon . . ."

CHAPTER 16

The men made it back to their campsite without any more obstacles, and now dusk was starting to settle in, so Eli began making a fire to cook the meat and vegetables they had brought. Lucas gathered scrub brush and limbs to set off to the side, making sure the fire would keep going for a while.

After dinner, they stoked the fire, and the tired men perched around the blaze on the two large rocks they had found nearby. They began talking about their backgrounds and what had brought them to this point.

Eli shared, "My father taught me that everything happens for a reason. When things went wrong in his shop, he would simply shrug his shoulders and say, 'As God wills it.'"

Lucas nodded in agreement. "It reminds me so much of my own dad. Whenever he faced difficulties, his words were always, 'It's not a big deal . . . unless I choose to see it that way.' Somehow or another, most of the things turned out fine—maybe because he chose to make them 'not a big deal.'"

Eli shrugged. "Makes sense to me." Then he looked at Lucas with a reflective expression, which had the young man wondering what was about to come next.

"Lucas, I want to share something with you. I think it's time."

Lucas's puzzled look did not go unnoticed by his mentor, so the cobbler continued. "You have said you want to be like I am when it comes to my philosophy and the way I deal with life and its challenges. You are the kind of person who will understand and appreciate what I am about to say—and very few people would be able to comprehend this."

The young Dutchman sat still and quiet, listening intently as the fire crackled in front of them.

"My father was a spiritual man, as was his father. Their work and their play each had a Divine element woven through them. My grandfather urged my dad to do everything impeccably. It was as if it was all part of his worship. He wanted to do things right because he wanted to honor God with everything he did."

Lucas nodded in agreement. "I love that."

Eli continued. "My father had a creed that he developed, and it was based on the traits he saw *his* father exhibit. It is a creed that has tremendous spiritual power."

Lucas cocked his head and raised an eyebrow in deep interest.

Eli reached into his shirt pocket and pulled out a faded piece of folded paper. "Here is a copy of that creed, Lucas. I keep it with me, and I refer to it every day."

Lucas's thoughts flashed back to the morning he walked into Eli's shop as the cobbler was reading to himself from what seemed to be the very same piece of paper.

This time, the cobbler unfolded it and began reading to Lucas . . .

THE COBBLER'S CREED

My life is one of gratitude for all that crosses my path.

Through patience, gentleness, enthusiasm, and love,

I see my journey as an inspired, opportunity-filled game.

In this game, there is no failure; there is only this:

Having great goals and great vision,
allowing them to be fulfilled,

Learning from the experience, and then moving on . . .

To the next great adventure.

At that point, Eli mindfully set the paper beside him and then slowly met the young man's eyes.

Lucas was noticeably moved as he spoke reverently to his mentor. "Eli, that is possibly the most beautiful thing I have ever heard. The carefully chosen words, the flow, the energy that emanated from it as you read . . . I've just never experienced anything like it."

Eli gazed into the distance, and the campfire lit up his profile. Then he turned back to Lucas and replied,

"Yes, the words have supernatural energy. You have asked how I am able to connect with people, to move them, to inspire them . . . it all starts with this creed. My philosophy of life, and all the beliefs I hold sacred, are captured in these tenets, which now permeate my spirit."

Lucas leaned back, crossed his arms, and exhaled. "Wow, it perfectly describes the way I see you live."

Eli smiled broadly. "Thank you. That is quite the compliment, and I am grateful." He then carefully picked up the paper and handed it to Lucas. "I want you to have this copy."

Staring in awe, the young man reached out and accepted the sacred item. "Eli, I don't even know what to say. I am so honored. But . . . why me? I don't feel worthy to receive something of this value."

Eli began speaking slowly and intentionally. "Lucas, for what we are doing, and will continue to do, we will *both* need the God-given strength inherent in this creed. Times are about to get very intense . . ."

Lucas held up his hand as if to stop him. "Wait, what do you mean '*intense*'? Eli, times seem to be great right now. Business is going through the roof, the community is thriving, people are happy . . . you and I are happy. So, why do you think times are about to get very intense?"

Eli looked up as if he were searching for precise words, then after a few seconds, his gaze returned to

Lucas. "Great success comes at a great price. Yes, we are laying the groundwork for amazing things. We are helping people see how they can bond together and transform tragedy into strength. It will take tremendous patience, yet at some point, there *will* be an unstoppable balance of power shift. But . . . there are also those who *aren't* so happy with us and with our community having success. There will likely be much more pain for us all before we reach our goal of equality and unity."

Eli noted the look of shock on Lucas's face. Trying to soften the conversation, he chuckled and quizzed him, "What is it, my friend?"

Lucas shook his head in apparent disbelief. "Eli, your words about some people not being happy with us . . . those were the same words of warning Victoria shared with me!"

Unfazed, Eli continued, "Well, she is right—and *she* should know."

"What do you mean by that?"

Eli addressed the young man firmly. "Lucas, she is the daughter of the Mayor of Cape Town. She knows things that you and I will never know. The fact that she was willing to share that with you and put herself at risk is unthinkably brave. Victoria clearly wanted you— wanted *us*—to be ready when the government decides to step in. Even though we are simply spreading goodness and empowerment throughout the community, this is terrifying to the South African politicians—because they know it will eventually lead to freedom for us all . . . not only in Cape Town, but in the whole country, and it could provide a model for others across the world."

Lucas nodded, now deep in thought, inspired by his mentor's passion and determination.

The men sat in silence as the sounds of the savannah played out around them. The hyenas yipped, the zebras whinnied, and the crickets chirped. It was like a symphony of wildlife as the fading fire continued to gently crackle.

Eli spoke softly and precisely, staring resolutely into the flames. "Just as there is great power in nature, as we hear all these animals harmonize in the African night, think if all our people could join in courage and faith and love. If everyone in Cape Town was unified in belief, the result would be a tidal wave of integrity that could not be overcome by guns and evil men. Those in power know it is true."

Lucas's eyes widened, and his pulse quickened. "Are you saying what I think you're saying?"

The cobbler's gaze fell to the fire, then he looked back into the eyes of the clearly inspired young Dutchman and shrugged. "I'm simply a cobbler, Lucas. But I do know this: *I have great goals and great vision, and I will allow them to be fulfilled . . .*"

Hearing Eli recite those words from *The Cobbler's Creed*, Lucas Van der Meer felt a chill run up his spine.

He folded the paper reverently, tucked it into his shirt pocket, and then spoke in a calm, unwavering voice.

"I'm with you to the end, Eli."

The gentle African smiled, nodded his gratitude, then gracefully reached for a nearby bucket of water to put out the night's fire. . .

CHAPTER 17

The pair spent the next day wandering the savannah, taking in all the magnificent sights. As they traveled across the land, Eli continued to share his wisdom, and the young man eagerly soaked it up. The cobbler's words seemed custom-made for Lucas, and the Dutchman's belief that this time in Africa was his destiny . . . was now stronger than ever.

When the morning of their departure arrived, Eli cooked some eggs and bacon over the fire, then prepared a pot of steaming coffee. After the scrumptious breakfast, Eli quietly took in the scenery one last time. Breathing in the fresh air of the grassland, he turned his eyes back to Lucas and offered, "Shabi will be at our meeting point soon, waiting for us, so we had better get going." The two men stood and cleaned up the site, then began gathering their belongings for the trip back to Cape Town.

A few moments into their packing, Lucas stopped, shook his head, and smiled at his friend. "Eli, I don't even know how to express my gratitude for you bringing me here. As strange as this sounds, I feel like I am a changed man for having been to this place." He then patted his shirt pocket containing *The Cobbler's Creed* and added, "Actually, I *know* I am a changed man."

Eli nodded in agreement. "That you are, Lucas. But don't forget, we've got a lot of work to do, and it will be anything but easy. However, you're now better equipped for the days ahead."

Lucas beamed.

After everything was packed up, the men headed south, hiking to the place where Shabi would connect with them. Along the way, they talked about the difficult journey so many South Africans would face in the days ahead. As they got closer to the meeting point with Shabi, Lucas asked, "Do you ever wonder why *we* were meant to do this? It is so humbling. . ." His voice trailed off.

Eli chewed on his bottom lip, thinking. "Plenty of people are chosen to do great things—and most think they are undeserving and incapable. However, we are *all* capable—no matter how unqualified we might feel. The reality is that even though many are called, few will answer. You and I answered."

Lucas smiled. "Yes, Eli . . . and I am grateful we did."

Just then, Shabi pulled up in his cab and steered slowly and carefully off the dirt road over to the meeting point the two men had just reached. He stopped, stepped out of the vehicle, and reached out to help with their belongings. "Fancy meeting you gentlemen here. Good sabbatical?"

Eli returned the smile. "Oh, yes, indeed. As always, I feel recharged—and ol' Lucas would probably tell you the same. Right, Lucas?"

Lucas grinned and nodded. "You can say that again. Plus, I have a whole new appreciation for large African snakes."

Shabi looked ahead and shrugged nonchalantly as all three men jumped into their places in the cab. "Well, I suppose that's a good thing—they definitely deserve respect." Then he glanced over his shoulder at Lucas and added with a chuckle, "Let's not even talk about the giant crocodiles."

Eli hit his open hand to his forehead in mock dismay. "Oh yeah, I guess I forgot to mention those, Lucas. They do tend to hang out around there."

Shabi and Eli laughed heartily as they saw their young friend playfully roll his eyes, then put his head in his hands. "Great. Just great."

The cab chugged on toward Cape Town as the men talked nonstop about their adventure in the savannah. They were so engaged, none of them could believe they had already completed the hours-long journey when the cab pulled up to Eli's home. Shabi got out and retrieved their luggage, and as Eli began reaching to hand him a tip, Shabi wagged a finger at him. "No, Boss, maybe next time." He smiled, shook Eli's hand, and then did the same for Lucas.

"It's been a pleasure," the driver added.

Eli and Lucas voiced their agreement, then Shabi tipped his hat, jumped back into the cab, and headed off to pick up his next customer.

Eli and Lucas walked up the short driveway, opened the front door, and headed to their rooms to get their personal items put away. After a few minutes, Eli looked at his watch and called back to Lucas, "How about if I make a couple of sandwiches, and we can take them back to the shop with us?"

Hearing that, the hungry young man darted down the hall, stuck his head around the corner, and gave Eli a thumbs up. "Sounds great! I'll be ready in a few minutes."

In less than half an hour, both men were fully unpacked, back out the door, and chomping on their sandwiches as they walked to the shop.

At one point, Lucas asked, "Eli, I know we are paving the way for something that is powerful for this whole country, but . . ."

Eli turned and cocked his head, wondering what the young man was about to ask.

"Does it not bother you to think that we may not be here to finally see the fruits of our labor—freedom and equality for everyone?"

Eli did not answer, and Lucas wondered if he had asked an inappropriate question.

Finally, Eli replied, "A man cannot always enjoy the fruit from the tree he plants, but still, if he knows in his heart he is being called to plant that tree for future generations . . . then he must plant."

Lucas persisted. "But what if the country just isn't ready for what we are doing?"

Eli shook his head. "As we discussed, you and I have chosen to answer a divine calling, although we don't know precisely how our roles fit into the plan. We may simply be the clouds preceding the great rain, but the clouds are necessary, too. That timing is in God's hands."

Lucas smiled and nodded, apparently satisfied with his mentor's answer. "I understand, Eli."

As they strolled past houses and shops, more and more people recognized not only Eli but now also his young assistant. They waved jubilantly and called out their adulation. "Eli! Lucas! Hooray!"

Lucas smiled sheepishly and waved back, then turned to his companion and grinned. "It's like we're celebrities. This is crazy!"

Eli stopped in his tracks. He turned, wagged his finger at the young man, and quietly but firmly said, "No, we are *servants*. Do not ever forget that. We are servants on a divine mission to bring desperately needed hope to people. As the Creed says, 'Through patience, gentleness, enthusiasm, and love . . .' That is what we are here to impart."

Lucas seemed to realize that he had overstepped his boundaries. "I'm sorry, Eli. I understand, and it will not happen again. Thank you for correcting me."

Eli offered a forgiving smile and patted the young man on the shoulder. When the shop finally came into view, they were both astounded by what they saw. Just in the few days since they had left, there was an extraordinary amount of new activity. More people, more construction, more positive energy. In fact, as they looked up the street, it was as if there was excitement as far as the eye could see.

"It's . . . wonderful," Eli managed to get out, fighting back tears. "It's exactly what I envisioned, and it's what everyone here deserves."

"You *knew* this would happen?" Lucas seemed baffled.

"Well, my friend, I believe there is a key ingredient in all of this. It's called . . . *faith*."

Lucas shook his head and smiled. "Yep, I think you're right."

As the men approached the shoe repair shop, the line there was long—and getting longer. It looked like it was going to be another great day—and another tiring one. They stepped up to the door, and right then, the African paused. It reminded Lucas of the time in the savannah when Eli happened upon the snake.

"What's going on, Eli? Hope it's not another one of those big vipers." Lucas smiled nervously.

Eli shook his head. "Much more toxic, I'm afraid."

The cobbler opened the door to his shop and immediately felt a sinking feeling in his stomach.

"Mr. Tambo, I am Mr. Botha from the Department of Native Affairs. This is my partner, Mr. Van Huber. May we have a word with you and your associate?"

Eli glanced at the clearly shaken Lucas, and then at the two tall, imposing white men in black hats and black suits. "I suppose so. You're already in my shop."

The man motioned to Eli and Lucas to sit in two chairs in front of the counter, which the officers had arranged. Botha began speaking as the cobblers sat quietly.

"Mr. Tambo, I suppose you know why we are here."

Eli grimaced, shook his head, and then replied, "Well, judging by your shoes, I would say you might need my services."

The man's eyes narrowed. "As you know, the laws of South Africa prohibit you from conducting any activities that may be deemed as disruptive to the state."

Eli nodded as Lucas, who was growing increasingly anxious, shifted his gaze between the two government officials.

The official added, "Well, I think you will agree that the mob you created in this area has the potential to cause problems for our government and our citizens."

Eli shook his head. "'Mob?' I think what you mean is that the government is threatened by the thought of people in this part of Cape Town becoming happy."

The other official started to move aggressively toward the cobbler, but Botha blocked him with his right arm. "I guess you can understand why my counterpart is a little bit on edge. He's very patriotic and doesn't respond well to threats on our nation's security."

At that second, Lucas instinctively stood up and blurted out, "He's done nothing but good—"

Van Huber quickly and harshly pushed the young man back into his chair.

Lucas shook his head and eyed the man with contempt as Botha continued his tirade.

"Furthermore, I understand that your associate has lured the mayor's daughter to this location, which of course you know is punishable for many reasons." At that point, the man pulled out a photograph of Victoria stepping into the cab from two days ago after visiting the shop.

Lucas's heart sank as he knew Victoria's visit was indeed forbidden, and it would be near impossible to convince anyone that she had come of her own free will.

Just then, Officer Botha said crisply to Eli, "If you and your associate will stand, I think it is time for both of you to come with us."

Eli knew any resistance at this point would be futile, so he and Lucas rose from their chairs, upon which the men each were gripped tightly by the shoulders and escorted out the door of the shop.

The cobbler was allowed to lock the door behind them, and as the four stepped outside, the entire street became silent. All the customers in line stared in astonishment. Then, those stares turned into glares of anger. Sensing more and more people coming over to see what the commotion was, the two officers abruptly pushed Eli and Lucas into the backseat of their waiting government car and began slowly pulling away.

As the increasingly larger crowd saw what was happening, the jeering started. Then, the jeers became louder while the swarm of people tried in vain to surround the car as it picked up speed and then began disappearing into the distance.

Eli looked back at the mass of people, then turned to Lucas. "This is where we must be stronger than ever."

Lucas was shaking, but as he saw Eli's calm demeanor, he remembered what the older man said after the incident with the snake. "*Everything that happens is preparing us . . .*" and he immediately felt a degree of peace, which surprised even himself.

Leaning toward the officials, Eli spoke. "I don't suppose you'll let us know where we are going, will you?"

Silence.

Eli nodded and leaned back.

About fifteen minutes went by, and the vehicle with its occupants pulled up to the three-story Native Affairs building, where a guard at the front gate stepped out to meet them. The driver rolled down the window and said in an annoyed tone, "I have some troublemakers."

The security officer peered into the back of the vehicle, then looked at the driver and his associate and motioned them through the checkpoint. A few seconds later, the car pulled into a parking garage under the building, and then swerved into the first spot, right beside an inconspicuous gray door. The two South African officers opened the car door for Eli and then for Lucas, and gruffly shoved them in the direction of the building.

Pointing to the entry, Van Huber huffed, "Over there."

Eli walked in first, followed by Lucas. As they entered the stark, dimly lit room, there was a man in a brown suit sitting behind a cherry-colored desk, which he was drumming his fingers on. He pointed to two rickety wooden chairs and ordered the two cobblers to sit down. As they did, Eli saw officers Botha and Van Huber now blocking the exit, arms crossed and with threatening looks on their faces.

The man behind the desk laced his fingers and leaned forward. He relaxed his clenched jaw and spoke in a tempered yet disapproving tone. "I am Schalk Van Pelt. So, you are Eli, the Cobbler of Cape Town . . . and this must be your associate, Mr. Lucas."

"If you say so, sir," Eli said evenly.

The man chuckled sarcastically. "Well, it's not just what I say. It's what the masses in District Six now say. But you see, there are problems . . ."

Eli cocked his head in anticipation.

"The first problem is that we are now seeing these 'masses' clogging our streets. This is unacceptable because crowds can quickly become mobs, Mr. Eli—especially if they are, shall we say, *influenced*. That is something we cannot tolerate, as it is not your place to brainwash citizens in a way that would be contrary to the aims of the South African government."

Eli and Lucas sat quietly as the man continued to build his case.

"Plus, there is another issue." He turned menacingly toward Lucas, then shook his head. "Mr. Van der Meer, it is my understanding that you have illegally lured a Caucasian woman into your district. Not only that . . . she is the daughter of the Mayor of Cape Town."

Lucas started to speak, but the man immediately held up his hand and continued. "Of course, you know the consequences of crossing these lines and attempting to fraternize with a woman of this stature."

"I did no such thing, sir." Lucas gritted his teeth and tried to mask his anger.

At that point, Van Pelt's lips drew back in a snarl, and he slammed his fist on the table. "Are you calling me a liar?"

Lucas calmly replied, "I am simply telling you the truth."

The man leaned back and laughed loudly. "*Your* truth doesn't count here, Mr. Van der Meer. Maybe back in Holland, but not in South Africa. We have numerous witnesses who stated they observed you with Victoria Lubbers. So, I will ask you . . . were you with her?"

"Yes."

Eli hung his head, sensing what was going to happen next.

The man stood up, leaned in toward Lucas, and shrugged. "Then, that is too bad. I'm afraid there is a large price to pay . . . for both of you." Van Pelt looked to the men standing by the door. "Take them away."

With that, the driver and his crony walked over to Eli and Lucas, plucked them out of their chairs, and led them out the door to the waiting car. The cobblers were pushed into the rear seat again, and the doors were closed, after which the car backed out of the garage and returned quickly to the gate.

The guard at the exit stepped to the driver's window as the car stopped. There were a few words exchanged, then the gate rose, and the car sped away.

At this point, Lucas and Eli had no idea where they were being taken. Lucas leaned forward and asked in a nervous tone, "Where are you taking us?" to which Botha replied curtly, "Where you both belong."

At that moment, Lucas Van der Meer wanted nothing more than to be back in Amsterdam. He wanted to be sitting with his mother and father, holding onto them like he never, ever had before.

But Lucas would never see his parents again, and he swallowed the lump in his throat as he realized he may never see *anyone* again . . .

CHAPTER 18

The government vehicle pulled up to a dilapidated stone building, which Lucas quickly realized was the Cape Town jail. With a sinking feeling, he intuitively knew what was about to happen—and there was no time or opportunity to reach out to anyone for help.

The two were briskly escorted from the car, down a short sidewalk, up two flights of old, creaking, wooden stairs, and inside the jailhouse. As they entered, an obese, bald man with rotting teeth was seated at a desk. Wearing a ragged, blue South African police uniform, he stood up and saluted the two men who brought the cobblers in. "I have their cells ready," he said with a smirk.

The officers nodded, and within thirty seconds, the cobblers were in separate cells, and anything that resembled freedom had been stolen away from Eli Tambo and Lucas Van der Meer.

With wide eyes, Lucas grabbed the rusty bars and looked through them at Eli. "I never dreamed this could happen," he breathed.

Calmly, the cobbler replied, "I always knew it could happen, Lucas. Now it has, and it is simply the next step on our journey. More than ever, it is time to think only thoughts of faith and strength."

Lucas slowly nodded to his mentor in understanding.

The two men sat down on their cots in silence, then in a few moments, Eli turned his gaze upward, smiled, and said aloud, "You know, Lucas, I sure would love to be back under those stars on the grassy plains, listening to the crickets and hyenas right about now."

"Well, it seems like we've got plenty of hyenas in our midst," Lucas replied with a nervous laugh.

Eli smiled and nodded, but he then seemed to slip deep into thought. "It's easy to be calm and trusting when things are going well, but when times like these test us, we must be patient and endure. Things will happen at the right time, just as *The Cobbler's Creed* suggests."

Lucas stood, gripped the bars again, and spoke in a heartfelt way to his mentor. "Eli, I admire you so much. I know you told me there were great prices to pay for great accomplishments, and you seem to have prepared yourself for that. I'm truly grateful to know you."

Eli flashed that big, comforting grin Lucas had come to count on. "The feeling is mutual, my good man. The feeling is mutual."

Two days came and went as the men remained in the dirty, decaying jail. Every few hours, a guard made his rounds, and twice per day they were brought meals—if one could call them such.

On the third day of no contact with the outside world, a guard came and opened the cell doors for each of the men. "You're going upstairs to see the judge," was the only explanation he offered.

Eli and Lucas obliged, standing, and then following the man up several more flights of rickety steps. They were led to another small, drab room where a frail-looking elderly man wearing a black robe and a gray, shoulder-length judge's wig sat behind a mahogany desk. He was leaning back, swiveling methodically in an oversized, cherry-colored chair, and his hands were laced tightly behind his head. "Ah, the cobblers have arrived," he said smugly.

Grabbing them by the shoulders, the guard planted the men firmly in front of the judge's desk, then he stepped back out of the room.

The magistrate took off his tortoiseshell reading glasses. "I understand you've been informed of the charges against you. They are quite serious," he scoffed.

Eli and Lucas both remained silent.

There was a lengthy pause, and then the man spoke again. "I want you both to step to the window with me." He rose from his seat, walked to the lone window in the room, and offered a sweeping gesture of the view.

What the two men saw when they looked outside seemed . . . *impossible*. There were thousands of people standing, chanting behind the razor-wired security fence. Their sound did not reach that drab room in the jailhouse, but the energy of the crowd was unmistakable.

"I don't understand," Eli managed to utter in disbelief.

The old man laughed and then screamed mockingly, "You don't understand? You don't understand?"

The man then abruptly raised the window, and the blaring noise was heard by the three men clearly: "FREE THE COBBLERS! FREE THE COBBLERS!"

Staring angrily at the crowd, the judge turned to Eli and Lucas. "*Now* do you understand? You two have caused me and many others great distress. Do you simply want to ruin this country, Mr. Tambo?" he protested loudly.

Eli looked at him and gently said, "Maybe the country needs to be 'ruined'—so that a country run by the will of *all* people can rise in its place."

He slammed the window shut. "Fools! That's what they are, and that is what you both are!"

Lucas stood quietly, shifting his eyes between the cobbler and the judge, now fully prepared to follow Eli's lead.

The justice gritted his teeth and then spoke harshly. "This match you have struck has started a fire that could grow into an unstoppable blaze. You have begun something that may change this country forever!" With that, he picked up his gavel and hurled it angrily at the wall.

Eli shook his head calmly. "No, sir, maybe we struck the match, but love has started this fire, and it will indeed burn with an unstoppable blaze—one that is so bright that not only Cape Town, but also the entire world, will see it."

Staring back out the window, the man chewed nervously on his lower lip and then alternated angry glares between Eli and Lucas. "Here are your options, gentlemen: to hang from the gallows in front of these thousands of people . . . or to address this mob and admit to them you have made terrible mistakes that have harmed the country, and you have decided it is in your best interest to leave. At that point you will be exiled, but free to go."

Seething with anger, young Lucas Van der Meer tensed his jaw and glared back at the robed man, who added coldly, "Either is fine with me at this point. Make your decision."

With no emotion showing, Eli turned to Lucas, noting the Dutchman's resolute countenance. Then the gentle, African cobbler looked back at the elderly judge and spoke with composure. "I would rather hang from the gallows than lie to the people who have believed in me. I would rather give my life knowing I have served our citizens to the end, rather than give them the belief that I have cowered in your cruel, unjust shadow."

The judge, trembling now with anger, nodded and then looked at Lucas with narrowed eyes. "And you, young man—what is your decision?"

Lucas felt his legs shaking. "I, sir, stand with The Cobbler of Cape Town—until the very end for us both."

The old magistrate turned away abruptly, then walked slowly back to his desk and eased himself into the chair. He paused, staring off into the distance, and then looked back and forth between the now steadfast men.

He put his elbows on the desk, laced his fingers together, and stared blankly at the wall, away from the prisoners. "Well then, I suppose this will indeed *be* the very end for both of you. We will prepare the gallows immediately, and you will be hanged at five o'clock."

Lucas Van der Meer fought back his tears as Eli turned to him and quietly asserted, "I am proud of you."

Staring callously at Eli and Lucas, the justice yelled for the guard, then shook his head slowly and mumbled, "Such a pity, gentlemen." Picking up a pen, he lowered his head and began writing the order of execution as the guard entered and took the two men back to their cells to await their chosen fate.

CHAPTER 19

The ticking of the clock on the wall seemed deafening as the seconds went slowly by. From their individual cells, both men glanced up simultaneously and saw it was now four o'clock sharp.

Lucas looked across at Eli. "One hour, my friend. One hour, and everything that we have worked for will be lost."

Eli's lips curled up into a slight smile as he shook his head. "Lucas, don't you understand? What we have done is give the disenfranchised citizens *hope*, which they have never had. We have managed to create change in thousands and thousands of lives, and there are people all over Cape Town who now believe in themselves. Plus, who knows the number of people who will be impacted through the powerful ripple effect? No, it is not loss, my friend . . . it is incalculable gain."

Lucas considered his mentor's words and then smiled broadly. "It's ironic, isn't it?"

Eli cocked his head in curiosity.

"It's ironic that I came to Cape Town wanting to make a difference, but with no idea what I would do, and with no idea where I would end up. You came here knowing exactly what needed to be done. Our dreams, different as they were, brought us together. Now it's a unified dream whose fulfillment will someday change the country . . . and maybe the world."

Eli nodded. "When God has a plan, it is simply up to you to say, 'Yes.' That is one thing you and I had in common from the very beginning—we said yes. From there, anything is possible."

Right then, the guard walked up to the two cells and spoke briefly and curtly to both men. "You will be escorted downstairs in thirty minutes. Prepare yourselves." With that, he turned and walked briskly away.

The men sat in silence for the next half hour, and then at the appointed time, they heard the door leading to the cell area opening, and they instinctively stood. But at that moment, the guard did not enter. Instead, Arend Lubbers, the tall, distinguished mayor, wearing a brown tailored suit walked up. Behind him was a woman that neither Eli nor Lucas would have ever thought they would see again.

"Victoria!" Lucas moved toward the cell bars and pressed himself to them as the young woman ran over and reached to clasp Lucas's outstretched hands. But when Victoria burst into tears, the mayor gently pulled her away and guided her off to the side.

To the surprise of both men, the mayor looked at Lucas, hesitated, and then began speaking in a calm, gentle tone. "My daughter has told me the story of the happiness you brought to her when she first met you." He then shrugged his shoulders and added, "You are all she has talked about since that time." He smiled.

The mayor then turned to Eli. "Mr. Tambo, you have been a very busy man." He smiled again. "Victoria has also told me about the positive impact you have had on the community where you live. I, on the other hand, have heard from many people in government about what a threat you are. I was informed of the impending execution, and I wanted to come meet you—and to meet Lucas also—before it was too late."

He raised an eyebrow at Eli and continued, "I must say, you and your associate do not look like threatening people. Are you?"

Eli smiled and gently offered, "Sir, I am simply a cobbler. My goal—and Lucas's goal—has been to make people happier, and to help them see that life is worth living. There's nothing either of us believe in more than doing this for the betterment of South Africa, and *all* its people."

The prime minister rubbed his chin and looked at Eli. "Just a cobbler, eh? I don't know many cobblers who have that kind of wisdom . . . and altruism."

Eli nodded affirmatively as the mayor then turned his attention to Lucas. "Lucas, is there anything you wish to say?"

Lucas looked down, and then brought his head up quickly. "Sir, I was raised in a family where love conquered all. Regardless of the pain people suffered—and I have suffered much—I was to believe that good would win out. I was taught that people are inherently good, yet people sometimes simply don't have all the facts. They don't have the ability to look at the perspective of others. What I would say to you today, sir, is that we are all searching for happiness. What Eli and I believe—and what I have shared with Victoria—is that we can all help each other find it. We all have gifts, and we all have dreams. When we can take those collective gifts, trust fervently, and then have a noble vision, incredible, even 'impossible' things can happen. This is what our mission has been: happiness and opportunity for all. Nothing more, nothing less."

Lucas glanced over and saw Victoria with tears rolling steadily down her cheeks. He turned away quickly, feeling his own tears welling up.

Furrowing his brow and staring intently into Lucas's eyes, the mayor seemed to be reflecting on the young man's words. Then after a few seconds, he gently clasped his daughter's hand and turned away. "Victoria, come with me," he said quietly.

The girl appeared confused as Mayor Lubbers looked back to the jailed men and added, "I shall be back in five minutes." With that, he and the young girl turned and walked out the door.

Eli sat down on his cot and looked at Lucas who had done the same. Both men stared at each other in disbelief.

"What . . . what just happened?" Lucas breathed.

Eli paused and then whispered, "I think you just gave a blind man a fresh view of the world."

Lucas shook his head gently. "We'll see, my friend . . . we'll see."

In five minutes, Mayor Lubbers returned, but was this time accompanied only by the guard.

"Open the cells, please." The guard nodded and hurriedly opened each of the cell doors, and the men stepped out.

Mayor Lubbers nodded at the guard, who then walked out and closed the door behind him.

The mayor looked away and then he looked back at the men and spoke cautiously. "Gentlemen, I would like to share something with you." Lucas and Eli each nodded tentatively. He continued, "Mr. Tambo, Mr. Van der Meer . . . my wife recently passed away."

Lucas glanced knowingly at Eli, but the African man's gaze remained fixed on Mayor Lubbers.

"I am sorry, sir," the cobblers replied in unison.

The mayor nodded in appreciation. "We had been married for thirty years. I had a dream as a young man of making South Africa into a place that people all over the world would admire. Instead, this beautiful land has become like a prison to so many South Africans. Not surprisingly, segregation is not working, as it is based on principles of hate and evil. Now I clearly see that is true, and my wife was finally able to see it before she died—in great part due to what Victoria taught us."

Eli and Lucas listened intently as the humbled man continued. "I am granting clemency for both of you, effective immediately. I don't expect anything from you in return, but I do not think it is safe for either of you to remain in Cape Town—or anywhere in South Africa."

Eli and Lucas appeared stoic as Mayor Lubbers carried on.

"At this point, most government officials and party leaders do not feel the same way I do regarding apartheid. Even though I do believe good will win out—as you so eloquently said, Lucas—I think it will be a long time before this full-scale change will happen in the country. Therefore, there will be many people who would try to stop what you are doing—and they have the power right now to do so."

The cobblers nodded.

"Gentlemen, I will help you with any obstacles you might encounter in exiting the country, but keep in mind, the stand I am taking will immediately put my own life at risk also."

With that, he turned and knocked on the door, requesting for the guard to reenter. As they waited, the mayor spoke again. "One last thing, Eli."

The cobbler arched an eyebrow and waited breathlessly. "Yes, Mr. Mayor?"

"I would appreciate it if you would do me a personal favor and address the crowd to let them know progress will be made—and ask them to disperse."

Eli looked into the man's eyes and saw the genuineness that radiated from them. "Yes, sir, I shall. Thank you."

With that, the guard escorted Eli and Lucas to a lower floor, taking them directly past Victoria, who was now standing quietly, holding a door open for them. That door, instead of leading to the gallows, opened to a different area overlooking the grounds outside the prison. There they saw a platform with a clear view out over the crowd, which the cobbler stepped up on, with Lucas remaining several steps behind, out of sight.

As soon as Eli was visible to the sea of people, the deafening cheers began. This continued for ten minutes, and then finally Eli raised his hand. Slowly, the noise abated, and the cobbler spoke gently, but with authority. "Ladies and gentlemen, I am honored you came to support me and Lucas today—I cannot even begin to know how to thank you."

Eli paused, looked out over the sea of people, and choked back tears. "Ladies and gentlemen, I am simply a cobbler . . ."

Again, the crowd roared its approval. Eli smiled broadly, and after about thirty seconds, he was able to continue. "But what I know for sure is that each of you has shown me today the power of coming together in love. When people enter our shop, my goal has always been for each person to leave happier and more fulfilled—and today I have proof that this has happened."

Again, the crowd thundered its agreement. After the noise subsided, he carried on. "I know that each of you wants those same things—happiness and fulfillment— for all people across our country, regardless of race or any other difference. I believe change is coming. It may not be as quick as we would like, but I now believe it *will* happen. In the meantime, what I would ask each of you is to treat each other in a way that continues this groundswell of love and hope. Encourage everyone you meet, answer hate with compassion, combat anger with kindness, and dissolve conflict with persistent love."

The crowd roared again, and then after a minute, there was silence.

"Lucas and I have been freed." Right then, Lucas stepped up to the stage to join him, and the two raised their hands in a show of unity.

Seeing both men together, the mass of people went into a jubilant frenzy. People were raising their arms in victory, dancing, and screaming with joy. After several minutes, Eli smiled and pleaded for quiet so he could continue.

"As I had prayed would happen, the fire of compassion and faith has been lit, and you all have demonstrated today that when we come together, the flames we fan can reach far and wide. Regardless of who we are or what our occupation is, we can each make a powerful difference. Now it is time to allow you to carry on with what Lucas and I have been blessed to start. It is time for the two of us to find a different path, and a different place, although each of you will always be in our hearts."

The audience was quiet as Eli continued. "I believe in each of you, and I believe in the future of Cape Town and all of South Africa, now more than ever."

One last time, the crowd screamed its approval. When the noise finally subsided, Lucas added, "Please, now, go home and hug the people you love, pray for our country, and remember that good days are ahead. Thank you, and God bless you."

Eli and Lucas stepped down from the platform until they were out of sight of the adulating crowd. They turned to each other and listened in gratitude to the applause one last time.

Walking back into the building, they saw the mayor standing just inside, waiting for them with an outstretched hand, which Eli and Lucas shook firmly.

"Thank you," the mayor said quietly to them both. Right then, Lucas saw Victoria walking from across the room toward them with a broad smile. Tears rolled down her cheeks as she first reached out and hugged her father. "I am so proud of you, Daddy."

The corners of the man's mouth turned up as he embraced the girl tighter. "Thank you, my dear. But I am so proud of *you*."

Victoria grinned, and then turned to Eli. "I am grateful for you, Mr. Tambo. You have walked in faith with Lucas and brought hope to thousands of people in this land." She hugged the man affectionately.

Finally, Victoria turned to Lucas, and her eyes twinkled as she said, "I cannot believe how fateful that first meeting between us turned out to be. You have been a rock for this community, and for Eli—and believe it or not—for me."

Lucas smiled as she continued. "When I met you that day on the boat, I could tell that God had given you rare gifts. I know the pain you have suffered, but I also know you have used that pain to develop an empathy that has already changed countless lives and has helped set the stage for what will eventually lead to change for the entire country. I know you must leave, but I only trust that when we meet again, it will be for a long, long time."

With that, she turned away from the others and cast a lingering gaze toward the blushing Dutchman.

Lucas looked lovingly at the young woman. "Victoria, your bravery is only outdone by your kindness. My life has been touched by you in a way that I cannot put into words. . ."

Right then, one of the guards entered and quickly said to the mayor, "The crowd has dispersed, sir. I believe I can now carry the men by car back to District Six." With that, he looked at the cobblers and then at Victoria. "We should go."

The two men nodded, and then once again they each shook the politician's hand. "Thank you, Mayor Lubbers. It has been an honor." Eli smiled as Lucas nodded his agreement.

The cobblers followed the guard out the door, and as they did, Lucas turned at the last second and saw Victoria's eyes focused on him, a tear rolling down her cheek. The young man waved one last time . . . and then disappeared out of Victoria's sight as the heavy door closed behind him.

Once they reached the floor where the car was parked, Eli and Lucas jumped in quickly as the guard took the wheel and began navigating the vehicle off the prison grounds. He gave a brief, validating wave as they reached the attendant to ensure the gate arm would rise.

It was a relatively short ride back, and the driver took them straight to Eli's home. Once they arrived, Eli and Lucas stepped out, closed the car door behind them, and started to walk away. Right then, they heard the guard's voice, and they turned and saw his window was now rolled down.

"Good luck," the previously bitter man now offered humbly. Eli and Lucas nodded their appreciation, and with that, he saluted the two cobblers and slowly drove off until the car was finally out of sight.

At that moment, the unthinkable fate they had just narrowly escaped occurred to the men at the same time. As the fatigued, peaceful warriors looked at each other with heavy eyes, Eli Tambo reached out and put his arms tenderly around young Lucas . . . and both men quietly wept.

CHAPTER 20

Drying their moist eyes on their sleeves, the men turned and walked up the steps to Eli's home. The ever-polite African opened the front door and gestured for Lucas to enter first. Eli followed and closed the door behind them. He walked to the kitchen and began preparing coffee as Lucas sat down at the kitchen table and stared blankly out the window.

Neither man spoke, but then Eli brought the steaming drinks over to the table and broke the silence.

"Lucas, what you did today was brave on a level that few people can even fathom. It was an honor to be there with you."

Lucas took a sip of coffee and then spoke slowly. "Eli, as you have told me and shown me, all things prepare us for a life of more strength and more courage. I don't know where those words came from today, but I know I wouldn't have owned them if I had not experienced all the events in my life—although I would not wish many of those events on anybody."

Eli nodded, amazed at the wisdom of his young friend. "Lucas, you have clearly absorbed and lived out the principles of *The Cobbler's Creed*. Indeed, The Creed is a part of you now. The personal power you have is indisputable, and the world will continue to benefit from that, wherever you go."

Lucas smiled. "Speaking of that, we both know the mayor is right—it is not safe for us to be in South Africa now as there will be targets on our backs. But who will carry on with our work?"

Eli nodded. "Yes, you're right, the time for us to leave is near." He paused and took another sip of his drink. "Two weeks ago, I received a letter from a young man I've been hearing about who is in school at the University of Fort Hare in the Eastern Cape. His name is Nelson, and he is intelligent, has excellent leadership credentials, and says he is eager to help shape the future of the country. I plan on reaching out to him as soon as possible, and if it goes like I hope it will, he will be the candidate."

Then, with a melancholy look, he added, "As far as leaving . . . I believe the proper time is tomorrow for you."

"What about you?" Lucas stammered. "I don't even know where I'll go, plus I won't leave without you, Eli."

The elder cobbler continued to sip his coffee, gazed out the window, and then looked back at Lucas. "You and I were brought together for a divine reason; we both know that. But our work here is finished, and we have laid the groundwork for great things in this country. I agree with the mayor; it will take time— maybe many, many years—but it will happen. Our role was to be catalysts by connecting the community and instilling belief in the people. Change can proceed now that these fundamentals are in place."

The cobbler gently continued. "As far as where you will go, I think you know in your heart what the answer to that is. It's time for you to go home, Lucas. You have helped change Africa like you assured your parents you would do. Your job is done, good and faithful servant." A smile spread across the weary cobbler's face.

Lucas nodded slowly, fighting back tears. "You're right, Eli. But the shop . . . and your home. What will happen to everything?"

Eli smiled, shook his head, and waved his hand dismissively. "All of that will be taken care of. I will close the shop in the next week or so, and as far as my home is concerned, it will sell quickly."

Lucas smiled back. "It makes me feel so much better to know you are not concerned. But, what about money? I'm not sure I have enough to even get back to Holland."

Eli paused. "That will be taken care of also."

Lucas raised a curious eyebrow as Eli continued. "Pack your things, get a good night's rest, and we will talk in the morning."

Nodding dutifully, Lucas then headed back to his room, wondering what the days ahead would hold for him. He packed a few items but quickly realized he was exhausted, and so he decided to wash up and turn in early.

The Dutchman, who had seemingly overnight gone from a wide-eyed European schoolboy to a courageous man whose work would profoundly impact Africa, lay down in his Cape Town bed one last time . . . and fell asleep as soon as his head hit the pillow.

CHAPTER 21

When Lucas awoke the next morning, he quickly realized he had slept better than he had in months. He knew his time in South Africa was coming to an end, but he now felt excited about the possibilities ahead. He jumped in the shower, threw on his clothes, and finished packing his last few personal items. After that, he walked toward the kitchen to see if his mentor was awake.

"Well, I'm glad to see you have joined the rest of the waking world," Eli's voice boomed as he heard Lucas coming down the hall, suitcase in hand.

Once the young man stepped into the kitchen, he saw Eli reaching out toward him with a large mug of fresh coffee and a big smile.

"Ah, just what I needed," Lucas happily sighed. He set his suitcase by the door, took the brew, and inhaled the aroma deeply.

Eli shook his head. "I knew that would be the case. It's been a long few days—to say the least."

Lucas nodded and grinned.

"I am going to head down to the shop now, my friend, and start telling folks about my plans. I know they will ask about you also." He pointed toward Lucas's luggage. "Judging from your suitcase, I'd say you're ready to go. I assume you've decided where you're headed?" Eli cocked his head in anticipation.

Lucas looked briefly away, and then turned back to his mentor. "If, as you said, money won't be a problem . . . I want to go back to Holland. I feel like I have healed so much—and I miss my homeland, Eli."

The cobbler smiled. "I had a feeling that would be your answer. I'm happy for you, and I do believe your longing for home is a sign the pain is subsiding."

The older man reached into his pocket and pulled out a pouch about the size of a marble bag. "This should be enough to get you home—or anywhere else." He held the bag out toward Lucas with a sly grin.

Lucas set down his coffee, and with a puzzled look, he reached out and accepted the gift, then slowly pulled the drawstrings open.

His eyes became like saucers as he poured the contents into his hand. "It's two pieces of . . . gold, Eli!"

The man laughed. "Yep, still can't slip a thing past you, can I?"

Lucas shook his head in disbelief and stared at the two chunks, each about the size of a small marble. "These have to be worth thousands."

Eli shrugged. "I think your estimate is a little on the low side, but either way, it will make things much easier for you. I have a friend who works in the mines, and he came across quite a few of these in a vein they discovered years ago. I didn't ask how he was able to keep them, but . . . he wanted to share them with me, and now I'm sharing with you." He smiled and winked at the young man.

Lucas placed the nuggets back inside the small pouch and then put it in his pocket. He reached out to hug his mentor and then pulled away slowly. "I will never, ever forget you, Eli. You changed me forever."

"It's been a privilege, Lucas." Eli offered a broad smile as he placed his hands affectionately on Lucas's shoulders. "Now, come on, let's go outside—I've arranged for a taxi to get you to the port, and it should be here any minute." With that, Eli reached down and picked up a carefully wrapped, fresh apple muffin and put it in Lucas's hand. "Can't let that bottomless pit get empty." His eyes twinkled.

Gratefully accepting the snack, Lucas picked up his suitcase, then turned and walked out the door, with Eli right behind. Breaking into a broad grin, Lucas immediately saw Shabi standing in front of his cab in the driveway. He tipped his cap to Lucas.

"I hear you need a ride!" He grinned, and as Lucas walked toward him, Shabi reached out and took the young man's suitcase, then placed it carefully in the back seat.

"You heard correctly, my good man. To the dock, please. I believe I can still catch the noon sailing if I hurry."

"Then you're wasting time. Let's go!" He closed the door for Lucas, jumped in the driver's seat, and slowly pulled away as his passenger turned and waved, watching Eli grow increasingly distant, waving back slowly and deliberately. *Goodbye, my mentor*, Lucas mouthed slowly.

In half an hour, the two reached the port, and Lucas looked up and saw the large ship looming in front of him about fifty yards away. He jumped out of the cab as it pulled up and came to a stop, grabbed his luggage out of the back, then walked around to the driver's side to pay Shabi.

The driver shook his head. "Consider this my farewell gift."

Lucas smiled. "What a great way to end my time here, Shabi. Thank you for everything."

The driver tipped his cap again, then reached out and shook the young man's hand. "It's a pleasure," he replied with a grin. After that, he started up the car and pulled slowly away as Lucas went to purchase his ticket and complete the papers necessary for departure.

Everything went smoothly in the exit process, and before he knew it, Lucas was on board for his journey back to Marseille, then home to Amsterdam. He took his suitcase to his room, unpacked, and then lay down on his bed to relax as he felt the ship slowly begin to pull away.

But after a few moments, he became restless. *Think I'll go up and watch as we leave port*, Lucas thought. *Seeing Africa one last time would be good for the soul*, he reasoned. He walked out of the room, locked the door behind him, and marched out to the deck.

Lucas could feel the warm South African sea breeze as he strolled. Once he reached the railing at the back part of the ship, he propped his arms on the rail to watch the continent fade into the distance.

Just then, his attention was drawn to a woman's tender voice coming from behind him.

"Care if I join you?"

Lucas turned away from his view of the shore and was overcome with emotion . . .

"Victoria! What . . . I mean, how—?"

The young woman placed her index finger gently on his lips. Giggling, she said, "Let me finish the sentence for you."

Lucas blushed as the girl playfully put her hands on her hips and continued. "'Victoria, I can't believe you would have even considered staying in Africa when you and I are destined to be together' . . ." She laughed.

Gaining his composure, Lucas joined in the fun. "Yes, and I was also about to say, 'How in the world will I explain how I was able to bring back the most beautiful woman in South Africa to one of the coldest places in Europe?'" He arched an eyebrow and smiled.

Her lips turning upward, Victoria gazed into the ecstatic young man's eyes. "Well, Mr. Van der Meer, I guess you'll just have to come up with an answer, because you're stuck with me—and that means for good."

Lucas persisted. "But, your father. How did he . . . I mean, how did *you* . . . ?"

Victoria held up her hand to stop him. "My father wants me to be happy. He said after the connection he saw between you and me that day that it was obvious we were meant to be together. He also knew I would not be safe now in South Africa, but he had no doubt I would *always* be safe . . . with you." She pushed her blonde hair back from her eyes and smiled broadly at Lucas. "Anyway, we've got a lifetime to talk about all of that. I say we just stand here and watch a beautiful South African sunset . . . one last time."

Lucas Van der Meer smiled, shook his head in disbelief, and then put his arms tightly around the young woman of his dreams as they blissfully watched the massive African continent dwindle to a speck on the horizon . . .

CHAPTER 22

The nurse looked in admiration at the elderly Dutchman and smiled. "What an incredible, beautiful story, Mr. Van der Meer! I'm truly honored that you chose to let me hear it."

Lucas grinned. "In the words of Eli Tambo, 'The honor is mine.'"

Isa was clearly touched. "Did you ever see Eli again after you left Africa?"

Lucas looked out the window, hesitated, then turned back to her. "We corresponded for a long time. After he left Cape Town, Eli spent the rest of his years living quietly in Tanzania, outside Dar El Salaam, where his family was originally from. He would write to me about the many long trips he took into the grassy plains there, like the one we took in the savannah."

The young woman's eyes sparkled as she continued to listen intently.

"At one point, he shared with me that he had become very ill, and I immediately got on a flight to Tanzania to see him. Gratefully, we were able to spend some wonderful time together on that trip before Eli passed away, three weeks later. Tomorrow is the anniversary of his death—fifty years ago."

Isa shook her head in sympathy. "I am so sorry, Mr. Van der Meer."

Lucas nodded his appreciation, but then his lips curled up into a slight smile. "Although Eli didn't live to see it, Nelson Mandela did an incredible job in leading the way to bring Eli's dream to fruition. After Cape Town and the whole country became unified, the success in South Africa stood as a beacon of hope for disenfranchised people across the globe."

Isa covered her mouth and rasped in amazement, "The world was literally changed . . . ."

The corners of Lucas's lips turned upward. "Yes, and I have no doubt Eli left this world a happy man, having selflessly softened the ground for that change."

Pausing and looking out at the sky, the Dutchman then added poignantly, "Eli once told me that when he died, he wanted to be buried in the savannah of Tanzania, in a beloved spot of his where he would 'forever be able to hear the songs of the hyenas and zebras.' My understanding is that's exactly what became of him."

Shaking her head in awe, the nurse then turned her gaze to the photograph on the nightstand of the beautiful, young, blonde-haired woman, seemingly in her thirties.

"Victoria was a beautiful woman, Mr. Van der Meer. I am so happy to hear how you two came together. It's a love story one could only dream of."

Looking over at the photograph, he beamed. "She was an angel. Her gentle spirit was unlike that of any person I have ever met—or ever will meet." Then his smile slipped as he added, "Losing her ten years ago to that horrid disease was something I have never gotten over. I can't wait until we are together again . . ."

Lucas's voice trailed off as he turned toward the window and stared at the increasingly cloudy Amsterdam day.

After a few moments, the nurse noticed the man's eyelids growing heavy. She touched him on the shoulder and offered softly, "Mr. Van der Meer, my shift is about to end. I'll be on holiday for a week, but I'll look forward to seeing you when I return. I do have lots of questions about the story—I can't wait for you to answer them for me." Her eyes gleamed.

Lucas managed a weary smile as his eyes began to close. "Yes, my dear. I shall look forward to that."

Isa pulled the bedspread up around him, then turned and walked quietly toward the door as the old gentleman fell sound asleep.

Turning back as she reached the doorway, she smiled and whispered toward the slumbering Dutchman, "Good night, Mr. Van der Meer . . .

CHAPTER 23

Seven days later, a renewed Isa de Wit walked into the lobby of the assisted living facility, and the uncharacteristically nervous-looking receptionist stepped out to greet her. "Hi, Miss de Wit, could you stop by Mr. Jansen's office? He'd like to speak with you before you begin your shift."

Isa raised a curious eyebrow at the woman, but then the nurse turned and strolled briskly down the hall until she reached the cracked door of the administrator's office. She knocked and then pushed the door open gently.

The middle-aged executive in a blue pinstriped suit swiveled his burgundy leather chair around, away from the window. He motioned for the woman to come in.

Still unclear as to why her presence had been requested, she stepped inside and asked, "You wanted to see me, sir?"

Gesturing toward a brown-and-cherry striped chair across from his desk, Mr. Jansen said dryly, "Please have a seat. I hope your holiday was pleasant."

Isa quickly noted how his neutral tone betrayed the well wishes. "Yes, thank you very much," she returned politely.

The man steepled his fingers and leaned forward until his elbows were resting on his desk. "I'm afraid I have bad news."

She narrowed her eyes and cocked her head, wondering what was coming next.

"One of your patients, a Mr. Van der Meer, passed away while you were gone."

Isa stood up with a distraught, disbelieving look on her face. "What? He was fine when I left . . . what happened?"

The man gave a half shrug and said somberly, "We're still not sure. It was less than forty-eight hours ago, and at this point, it seems his heart simply gave out. He mentioned something about 'Victoria' when one of the nurses went to check on him in the middle of the night, then he became more vocal, although quite incoherent. He passed away shortly after the nurses tried to wake him."

The young caregiver put her head in her hands and sobbed quietly.

Shaking his head, the administrator added sympathetically, "I'm sorry, Miss de Wit. Although a caretaker can bring happiness into people's lives, the job is certainly painful sometimes."

With tear-stained cheeks, Isa slowly raised her head as he continued. "Mr. Van der Meer left something under his bed—a shoebox—and it had your name on the outside."

With that, he reached down into the lower right drawer of his desk and retrieved a worn box, with *Miss Isa de Wit* scribbled across the lid. He handed it across the desk to her and quietly assured her, "No one has opened it."

Swallowing the lump in her throat, Isa reached out to accept the container. Sitting back in the chair, she carefully removed the top and peered inside at the contents. The first thing that caught her attention was an envelope with her name on it, taped to the top of a smaller box about the size of a ring box.

She opened the envelope, then removed and unfolded the weathered paper inside, and surveyed the words of the title . . . *The Cobbler's Creed*. It was undoubtedly the original document that Eli had given to Lucas, but there was a change—the grammar had been altered in pencil by Lucas to reflect *past tense*.

Looking up from the text, Isa placed her hand over her mouth and fought back the tears. Then a few seconds passed, and she returned her gaze to the page to begin reading aloud . . .

The Cobbler's Creed

My life was one of gratitude for all that crossed my path.

Through patience, gentleness, enthusiasm, and love,

I saw my journey as an inspired, opportunity-filled game.

In this game, there was no failure, there was only this:

Having great goals and great vision,
allowing them to be fulfilled,

Learning from the experience, and then moving on . . .

To the next, great adventure.

At the bottom of the page, she saw the kind gentleman had written a personal message to her, which she continued to read aloud:

"Now, Miss de Wit, I sense the time has come for me to move on to my next great adventure. I am grateful to have met you, and I trust my gift will make your life even better as you continue to make a difference in the world . . . 'one person at a time.'

Your friend,

Lucas"

With tears now streaming steadily down the young nurse's cheeks, she reached into the shoebox and pulled out the smaller container. She opened it with trembling hands, and her eyes widened when she saw the contents—a marble-sized nugget of South African gold, surely worth a small fortune.

Wiping the corners of her eyes, Isa looked up at the deeply moved administrator, who shook his head and softly uttered, "This man . . . must have been special."

Lowering her gaze back down to the shoebox, then to the tear-stained paper, the young woman shook her head and slowly lifted her eyes back to him, replying delicately, "Sir, in all due respect, Lucas was not just *special.*" Then after a lengthy pause, she raised her chin and added, "Lucas Van der Meer helped change the world . . . and he made me believe *I* can do the same thing."

Rising from the chair and then gathering her new belongings, Isa smiled, turned away, and walked quietly out the door to begin her morning shift . . .

Find more inspirational stories from Skip at
www.skipjohnsonauthor.com

AUTHOR'S NOTES

The Cobbler of Cape Town was one of the most challenging—and subsequently fulfilling—fiction books I have written.

The difficulty in writing about South Africa for me is that it is an incredibly complex country. The complicated political history, the varied people groups, and the problematic, long-standing issue of apartheid, along with my initial unfamiliarity with the country, made it a tricky task.

"Then, why write about it, Skip?" you may ask.

Here's why . . .

If you're acquainted with my writing, you know I typically write stories that are set in exotic, faraway places. Africa is a continent I have wanted to use as a setting, and after I researched several countries in it, I narrowed the specific location down to Morocco or South Africa.

I have always been fascinated with South Africa and its diversity. I love the animals, the rugged beauty of the savannahs and plains, and the stunning southern beaches. The more I researched the country and its history, the more intrigued I was.

It was my front-runner.

Around that same time, I received an inspiring email from a loyal reader named Lynn Storen. She suggested I consider seeking out ways to use my writing to address social issues or to bring some healing to people or groups from a global perspective. I loved her idea, and again, South Africa seemed like a good place for this.

What "closed the deal" was this: Just before I was scheduled to start writing, I went to pick up some shoes at a small shoe repair shop in the city of Peachtree City, Georgia, near where I live. The job I gave the cobbler was a difficult one, and when I picked up the shoes, I was amazed at the perfection of his work. When I shared my appreciation with him, he gave me a big smile and a heartfelt thank-you in return. I left the shop feeling happy, he clearly felt good from the genuine compliment, and the energy of this simple transaction between us seemed to have a spiritual context to it.

Consequently, I went home and jotted down a one-page short story about a mystical shoe repair shop. I called it *The Cobbler of Cape Town*, since I had South Africa on my mind, plus it seemed to have a nice ring to it. I liked the story, so I sent it to my parents who also liked it, and . . . *The Cobbler of Cape Town* was born. I hope you enjoyed it!

MAY I ASK A FAVOR?

Thank you for reading my book! Would you do me a favor and take a moment to write a short review on Amazon? Reviews are extremely important to authors like me, and if you would share your thoughts so others can find out about my writing, I would be truly grateful.

If you leave a review, feel free to let me know by dropping me an email at skipjohnsonauthor1@gmail.com so I can personally thank you.

Who knows, maybe you'll even have an idea that will make it into my next book!

WANT TO GET WEEKLY INSPIRATION FROM ME?

To get new, weekly inspirational stories and articles at no charge—and to stay updated on my release dates for new books—send an email request to me at skipjohnsonauthor1@gmail.com. I'll also send you a free inspirational e-book of mine as a thank-you!

ABOUT
SKIP JOHNSON

Skip Johnson is an award-winning inspirational author whose goal is to empower, inspire, and enrich the lives of his readers.

He is known for his easygoing style of adventurous storytelling, with rich elements of spirituality, mysticism, and personal growth woven throughout his books. One prominent aspect of Skip's writing is how he takes readers on symbolic journeys of self-discovery and enlightenment. His characters often find themselves on treks to faraway places where meetings with wise, mystical mentors lead readers to contemplate their own personal and spiritual journeys and how their lives can be more fulfilling and joyful.

His storytelling is simple yet profound, allowing readers from all walks of life to extract and quickly apply the nuggets of wisdom, compassion, and peacefulness that permeate the pages of his narratives. He uses crystal-clear imagery to create the feeling for readers of being right beside each character on their life-changing, heroic journey in every saga.

Skip's books are both spiritual and practical. Each story encourages readers to look inside themselves for the magic, courage, and strength that is often deeply hidden within themselves, patiently waiting to be released to powerfully impact the world.

Based in Georgia, Skip himself has traveled many paths, including that of a motivational speaker, a business leader, a master tennis professional, and a world traveler. These experiences have shaped his writing, and the wisdom and insights woven into each story leave readers filled with wonder, gratitude, and enthusiasm for the days ahead.

In addition to *The Cobbler of Cape Town*, Skip is the author of the novels *The Mystic's Gift*, *The Gentleman's Journey*, *The Treasure in Antigua*, *The Lottery Winner's Greatest Ride,* and *The Statue's Secret*, as well as the nonfiction books *Grateful for Everything, Hidden Jewels of Happiness,* and *Starting Each Day in a Powerful Way*. His works have earned the Maxy Awards Book of the Year, the International Book Award, and the Nautilus Silver Award.

Made in the USA
Columbia, SC
12 November 2023

25409226R00109